PUZZLE
OF
MURDERS

*Jef,
Thank you for following my art over the years.*

Brandon Pitts

BookLand press

TORONTO, CANADA

Copyright © 2011 by Brandon Pitts

All rights reserved. No part of this publication may be reproduced or transmitted in any form or by any means, electronic or mechanical, including photocopying, recording or any information storage and retrieval, without the written permission of the publisher.

This book is a work of fiction. Names, characters, places and incidents are either the product of the author's imagination or used fictitiously, and any resemblance to actual persons living or dead, events or locales is entirely coincidental.

Published by BookLand Press
6021 Yonge Street
Suite 1010,
Toronto, Ontario, Canada M2M 3W2
www.booklandpress.com

Printed and bound in Canada.

Library and Archives Canada Cataloguing in Publication

Pitts, Brandon, 1967-
    Puzzle of murders / Brandon Pitts.

ISBN 978-1-926956-07-7

    I. Title.

PS8631.I882P89 2011   C813'.6   C2011-906199-6

Preserving our environment
Bookland Press chose Legacy TB Natural
100% post-consumer recycled paper for
the pages of this book printed by Webcom Inc.

MIX
Paper from
responsible sources
FSC® C004071

TABLE OF CONTENTS

CHAPTER 1	5
CHAPTER 2	10
CHAPTER 3	15
CHAPTER 4	21
CHAPTER 5	27
CHAPTER 6	34
CHAPTER 7	39
CHAPTER 8	49
CHAPTER 9	54
CHAPTER 10	59
CHAPTER 11	63
CHAPTER 12	69
CHAPTER 13	73
CHAPTER 14	76
CHAPTER 15	81
CHAPTER 16	86
CHAPTER 17	94

CHAPTER 18	99
CHAPTER 19	107
CHAPTER 20	115
CHAPTER 21	119
CHAPTER 22	121
CHAPTER 23	127
CHAPTER 24	134
CHAPTER 25	140
CHAPTER 26	144
CHAPTER 27	150
CHAPTER 28	154
CHAPTER 29	158
CHAPTER 30	162
CHAPTER 31	166
CHAPTER 32	173
CHAPTER 33	177
CHAPTER 34	185
CHAPTER 35	192
CHAPTER 36	196
CHAPTER 37	203

CHAPTER 1

MY EARLIEST MEMORIES were of Sunday school, listing to the story of Abraham and Isaac- about how God had ordered him to kill his son. Before this, I remember nothing. It's as if I never existed, as if I showed up one day, occupying this body. My thoughts were without shape or form, floating through the void, wrenched in nothingness. Only vague spheres were my friends.

I remember sitting in Sunday school, feeling as though I had been there, watching Abraham holding the knife, ready to slit his child's throat.

The vision was as real as a memory. I could see it. On top of the hill was a large stone that had fallen from heaven, a meteorite. There were green trees and patches of grass. Abraham had laid his son on the stone and offered up a prayer, then held the knife over the lad's neck. I remember standing behind him, grabbing his hand.

"What are you doing?" I said to Abraham.

"God's will," he said, with tears in his eyes.

"Who are you, to deny this boy a future and rob him of his sentience?"

From there, the vision faded.

I raised my hand.

"Yes, Sam," said the Sunday school teacher.

"It wasn't Isaac," I said.

"What do you mean?" said the teacher.

"It wasn't Isaac. Abraham took Ishmael up to Mount Moriah to sacrifice, not Isaac."

The teacher sat there, thinking for a moment before responding. "No, Sam. The bible tells us that it was Isaac whom God ordered Abraham to sacrifice, not Ishmael."

"God didn't order him to kill his son. That's why I grabbed his hand, holding it back. And that's how I know it was Ishmael."

After that day, I quit believing in God. The question of God never came up again until I decided to kill Steve Jahl, after he had rapped my sister.

It's funny, in my hour of need; I instinctively reach for you as I fall. Lord, I was going to ask for mercy. But after Steve raped my sister, I had an itching need to touch his body and feel it turn cold as his life force left him.

In my daydreams, I would murder him slow, nothing crude or hasty. Quite awful for him, but it would be the only beauty he would ever know.

So just like Abraham, prepared for the sacrifice, I sat down on Christmas Eve and leaned my back against a rock that would serve as Steve's headstone, pondering life before his acquittal.

Steve had given up on school the day he turned sixteen. Mopping floors had financed his Plymouth Duster, which in turn furnished Steve with knowledge in the arts of the wrench. This knowledge provided his father, who drove a garbage truck for the city, with a false optimism that the wrench would one day help Steve rise above his janitorial position.

Oh the power of the wrench!

He was the janitor at my sister's school so in my mind, this made the crime all the more severe. Steve was my age, only twenty but old enough to get hired on.

On the day Amanda got raped, she was hanging out with Steve's pubescent slut of a sister, Lily. Though her indiscretions seemed to know no limits, she managed to conjure scruples when it came to her brother's sexual advances.

"Perhaps if he were hot," she confessed to a friend, but Steve lacked the visage and physique necessary to inspire incestuous attraction.

He had curly hair and a look of stupidity that resembled artistic renderings of the homo-erectus, 'cept Steve was a little more slouched over. He would lean on his mop handle, leering at the teenage girls who wandered the halls of Fairdemidland High. The kids used to call him "Jocko Homo" and "Mongoloid."

I pulled up to Steve's house at 496 Malchut Street. A piece of crap castle made of wood and plastic siding, hovering over a basement, and surrounded by a moat of browning grass. Their father was out front in his wife beater.

"Hey young man," he said. "Got a new van?"

"I wouldn't call it new. Just bought it used. I'm here to pick up Amanda."

"Think they're around back. If you see Lily, tell her I'm going to Mickey D's to bring back some supper."

I looked at his greasy long hair and enormous beach ball paunch and walked through their dead lawn to the backside of the A-frame house. There was Lily; all thick legged with blonde hair and fat ass. I had lusted after her all through school but to no avail- seems she's gone out with everybody but me.

"Hey Lily."

Stepping on her cigarette, she barley acknowledged me, the vibes cutting between us like an unwanted wind.

"Where's Amanda?"

"I think she's in the basement with Steve."

I found this odd. Amanda hated Steve.

"He stares at me in between classes at school," she would say, "always cleaning up some mess by my locker.

It's really creepy. I hate going over to Lily's. Even her dad is a slime."

Lily went to the back door and yelled down for Amanda. My gaze followed her skintight white cotton shorts and her robust shanks. She stood halfway through the doorway, waiting for a response and then went down stairs.

I turned to look around their back yard. Artifacts from Steve and Lily's childhood were strewn around the property. Rusted bikes & toys, and an above ground pool, half covered, half full of leaves and algae water.

Amanda and Lily emerged from the dungeon. My sister was crying, her eyeliner sliding down her face and her hair loosed from her ponytail.

"What's wrong?"

"Nothing." She avoided eye contact, shaking her head and waving me back with her hand.

"She's fine," said Lily. "Aren't you?"

"What's been going on down there?" I said.

"Nothing. She was fooling around with Steve when she shouldn't be."

"I'll kick his ass if he's touched my sister."

Lily put her hands on her hips and stepped forward. "It's her fault, not Steve's."

"Let's go," said Amanda. "I just want to leave."

We got into the car and pulled off. Amanda refused to look at me and turned the radio up, full volume.

"What was all that about?" I asked, turning it back down.

"Look, I don't want to talk about it."

She rested her face into the palm of her hand, pretending to look out the window. Tumble weed and sage, nothing to stare at. I tried to remain silent but a burning need to know coursed through me as I drove my van out onto the bypass.

"What were you doing with Steve? You told me you thought he was a creep."

"Shut up Sam." Amanda started to cry again.

It wasn't until the following day that Amanda came forward, stating that Steve had raped her in his basement. Seems his mother; father and sister were watching TV upstairs, ignoring her screams for help - even during commercials.

CHAPTER 2

THE NEXT MORNING my mother called the cops. I'd experienced the police before. But this was the first time I hovered around them, sniffing out their vulnerability. I was the one who answered their knock on the door, inspecting their subtleties and weaknesses.

"Hello? We're here to speak with Miss Amanda Giltine."

The cop stood in the shade of our awning, hiding behind dark glasses and a bulletproof vest. His partner looked the same but was chewing gum.

"Come in." They walked past me. I shut my eyes and could hear their hearts beating, sensing their attitudes toward my sister. My mother beckoned them to sit down.

"Miss Giltine, can you tell us what happened yesterday?"

"I went to visit my friend Lily Jahl and her brother Steve forced himself on me in their basement." She began to cry.

"Where was Lily when this happened?"

"Upstairs watching TV with her parents."

The policeman looked up from his notepad. "That's funny. Your friend Lily and her father claim they were talking with your brother outside, in the yard, while you were in the basement with Mr. Jahl. Are you quite certain that they were upstairs in the living room during your time in the basement?"

"Yes. They must have gone outside during the rape. My brother was out back with Lily when I came up."

"So you're corroborating Miss Jahl's story?"

"Yes but all three were watching TV when I went into the basement."

"Why did you go down into the basement alone with Mr. Jahl?"

Amanda went silent.

"Is Steve Jahl your boyfriend?" the policeman asked pointblank.

"No," she cried, hitting her thigh with a fistful of tear soaked tissue. "He raped me and stalked me at school."

The officer raised his brow and looked up from his notepad. He was a typical country cop, beef fed and fibrous, fresh from the glory of high school sports, yet still a few years away from a pot full of guts under that bulletproof vest.

"He claims that the two of you were out on a date and that he thought you were eighteen. I mean you turn eighteen in what, three weeks?"

"Do I look like I would date a monster like Steve Jahl?"

"We do have a witness that says she's known you for years and claims you'd date just about anybody."

"Go away," cried Amanda.

"Maybe we'd better try this again later," said my mother, smiling at the policeman, trying put on a show for good impression.

"Ok," he scowled, glancing at me out of the corner of his eye, stuffing his notepad into his pocket. "Here's my card." He handed it to my mother.

I watched them leave, certain they would pay for what they'd done in life.

Amanda sat on the couch, crying. I went to touch her shoulder but she shooed me away. Silently, I left. I had plans to meet my buddy, Ted Salinger, at the Toad Bucket Café anyway.

The café was located in the parking lot of this automated gas station but was real swanky inside with naugahyde chairs and earthen tiles. Ted wasn't so into the coffee thing, preferred beer. We always met at the bucket because he dug on the chicks that worked there.

Sure the chicks were cool but I hit that place every day and didn't want these broads thinking I was a creep. Ted didn't mind what they thought, but I did.

We sat talking, barely aware of our surroundings until I was startled to see a black mug placed before me. I looked up. It was Janet, a girl so beautiful, that I was certain she were an angel of mercy, bringing me my cappuccino.

"Here you go, Sam."

"Thanks Janet."

"Your friend's mocha is coming right up."

"Wow," said Ted, "she's got to be the hottest girl in Fairdemidland."

"Yeah, she's pretty fine," I quickly agreed, hoping he'd keep his voice down or change the subject.

One reason Ted didn't care about what these girls thought was that he was dying, or so he said. If his tenure on this earth was to be cut short, he was damn sure that etiquette wouldn't get in the way of his zeal for a fine girl like Janet. Janet took it in stride and went back to her espresso bar.

Ted had diabetes bad, made worse from dope. The doctors had given him six months to live if he didn't give it up. He just couldn't stop himself.

"I sure would like to make it with a chick like that before I die," he said, turning around in his seat to look at Janet.

"Yeah, good luck. Better think of something else for your dying wish."

"There is one other thing I want to do before the grim reaper takes me," said Ted, looking down at his whipped cream without guilt or concern for his health. "When I know I'm about to go, I'm gonna walk into the Fairdemidland police station with a gun and shoot every cop I see."

"Wow man, that's a little dire."

I sipped my latte and my glance landed on Janet. Ted was a fool about some things but he knew true beauty. She was pretty special but she was no Lilith Jahl.

"Why waste bullets on Fairdemidland cops?" I said.

"Because they're a bunch of assholes. They're supposed to serve and protect, instead they just harass the youth. They're worthless. You were just telling me about that dick that was investigating your sister's case. He won't help your sister. He thinks she's a slut."

I was beginning to get angry.

"I say we take the law into our own hands," said Ted, "and kick Steve Jahl's ass."

His words pierced deep. "Or murder him," I said.

I sat, stunned by my own statement. It was a shocking revelation, a glimpse into my deepest recesses, as if my subconscious mind knew I was capable of such a thing.

"Or murder him," said Ted, sitting back into the black faux leather chair, oblivious to the look of guilt on my face. "A vigilante would be far more effective than these cops." He swatted the air with his hand. "You could be like a guardian of the community up in his watchtower. Nobody fucks with a vigilante."

I stared into my coffee, thinking about how much I'd like to kill Steve. "We better just let the cops do their job, see how it goes."

"Whatever man."

I coughed violently into my fist.
"Are you ok?"
"I'm getting sick. Maybe you're right," I said. "Maybe I should consider murdering the entire Jahl family, even Lily."
"There you go." He sat back, laughing.
But could I kill her?
I don't know, I thought. I just don't know.
Do it, said my voice of reason.

CHAPTER 3

ON DECEMBER 23rd they acquitted Steve Jahl. This made Christmas Eve especially painful, so I went to Ted's to ease my burden.

Ted had a trailer down by the river where poor people lived who filled their yards with parked cars that didn't run. I sat on the couch in his living room where the carpet was worn to the mesh. Beer cans littered the pressboard coffee table where he weighed his pot and rolled his spliffs.

"Ted, I can't help it, I'm stuck on this girl Lily and I feel so guilty about it."

"Dude," he said, licking the interleaved paper of his joint like *Le Zouave*. "Her brother raped your sister."

"I know."

"She's no good, Sam. There's at least a hundred other girls a notch above Lily Jahl- right here in Fairdemidland."

He lit up and passed the chillum. I took a drag and the smoke scraped my throat, burning my lung.

"I know," I said, holding it in. "I can't help it. It's just everything about her- her ass & legs and the motion of her walk- I even like the way she talks."

"Good God Sam, have some self respect. These folks have harmed your family in a terrible way. Besides, the girl's a whore and will probably look like her mother by the time she's old enough to drink."

"My heart yearns for this Lily girl. In my eyes, she's perfect. If you could freeze her in time, right here, at this moment, she might be a masterpiece for the ages. I could put her on the mantle next to my grandmother's ashes. In my sight, she glows and that makes it all the harder."

Ted sat on the couch, looking at me like I was an apparition. "Wow man. I don't know what to say. You better pull yourself together."

"Can't help it. She's seized the reins of my deepest desires. Why did the brother of the girl I love have to go and rape my sister? The whole time I sat across from her in the courtroom, I felt guilty- wanting to hate her but I just couldn't."

"Have you talked to her?"

"No. I've never really talked to her. At the trial, she just sat there, picking grime out from under her fingernails and whipping it on her pants. It doesn't matter. To me, she's a treasure, a find, dug up from the sands of Jericho and placed in some museum to show us how the ancients lionized fertility."

"Jesus, Sam, get over it. She's no good."

"I know. She's fucked everyone in town but me. She's such a slut; it's like being the only fool to not lucky enough win the lotto pot."

Ted stood up and dusted off his pants. "After this conversation, I need a beer. Let's go and visit Charlie."

Charlie was a guy who sold weed and other such wares. He was Ted's connection.

When we got there, Charlie opened his door, looking like Jesus or Jim Morrison when he had a beard. His whole house smelled like pot.

"Ted, Samael, how is it?"

"Charley."

He led us into his living room and we sat on a worn couch. Charley passed us a fancy blue and red colored bong that gurgled and burped when you took a big hit. His walls had this dark faux wood paneling, the kind you used to see back in the day. They were covered in psychedelic posters and a large Confederate Flag.

"What's up with you guys?" said Charlie, loading the bowl.

"Oh, Sam here's been telling me how he's stuck on that slut Lilith."

"Lily Jahl?" He handed the bong to Ted, holding in his breath as he spoke. "Poke her for me, will ya, Sam?"

"He can't," said Ted, motioning with Charlie's dark blue bic lighter. "She won't have anything to do with him and after the scandal with Sam's sister, well, you know."

Charlie began to cough on his *hit*. "She won't do him because she only fucks for drugs. Get her high, Sam."

"I don't know. I want her to like me for me."

"Shit," said Charlie, blowing out the smoke.

"That's what I'm saying, Charlie, Sam's in love with this girl."

"Wow, man."

"Say buddy," said Ted, "got any Miller High Life?"

"I got *mota*, *whack*, all the high life you need."

"Yeah, I'll take a *ball* off you, but maybe we could stop by 7-11 for some beer."

"Sure. Let's just settle, then we'll hit the *Sev*."

I got up to leave Ted and Charley to their wickedness.

"Where are you going, Samael?" said Charlie.

"I'm going to take a long walk and think about the happier times of Christmas past. Maybe I'll climb *Camelback Mountain*."

"Suit yourself," said Ted. "Crazy motherfucker."

I stopped at home, put on a Levis jacket and grabbed a bottle of JD. I drove out of town as far as the road would take me and parked next to a frozen irrigation canal at the foot of the mountain. Stepping out, I looked to my left. Leaning against the passenger seat was a shovel, left over from when I helped my mom plant winter cabbage in her yard. It had been there for weeks and I was too lazy to put it away.

Take it, I thought. Take it and dig a grave.

I paused for a moment, then grabbed the shovel and a can of spray paint, jumping across the irrigation canal. It was cold. I wished I had worn a heavier coat.

The grade up the mountain was so steep that when you tilted your head all the way back, the mountain summit filled the horizon. It was a large treeless wonder. I pulled myself up with my hands. Tumbleweeds and sage poked me and grass seed stuck to my sox. I looked around, unable to decide if the fauna was a shade of green or just brown.

It was half way up the mountain when I began to cough. Not the smoker's sort but that deep wet kind that makes grandmothers nervous.

When I reached a plateau, the ground formed a natural basin that shielded the view from below and vise versa. I needed to rest so I sat against a rock, wheezing and shivering. The only sound was my breath and the wind.

I remember thinking that if one were to become injured and stranded out here; no one would ever find you.

Then it hit me! I'd found the spot for Steve's grave. My skin bristled at the thought and butterflies erupted in my stomach. I felt the gross exaggerated sensation of my hair being blown by the wind. It stung, because the skin that covered my skull had become numb and bristled with excitement.

Taking a swig of Jack Daniels, I began to realize how cold it was. Determined not to give up, I wiped my nose with the back of my hand and stood up with resolve, slamming the blade of the shovel into the dirt at my feet.

It was sheer ecstasy, feeling the earth split so I started to dig with fury. The physical sensation of drawing soil from the ground gave me the feeling of superiority and made my desire to kill Steve tangible in the tactile sense.

The deeper I dug, the more I began to understand that what I was doing wasn't really vengeance. It was something more. It was justice and I could feel it in my hands in the form of the shovel's wooden handle.

"Fucking impotent cops and prosecuting attorney," I shouted into the wind. "I'll get the job done. Just give me duct tape; some rope and a t-ball bat."

By the time it began to snow, the brim of the hole reached my upper thighs. I began to sweat and my nose was secreting a thin saline type liquid all over my upper lip that I wiped dry at regular intervals.

I increased the intensity of the dig, determined to finish before the setting of the sun robbed me of what little warmth it offered. The hole was coming along. When I stood, my chest was now at ground level. I began to cough violently and dropped the shovel, falling to the ground in a ball.

I had to finish. The state had their arraignment on this day and I, the higher form of justice must have mine! But this time there'll be no acquittal. That's how it is.

Laying in the hole all curled up, I basked in the symbolism. The laymen were at home celebrating the birth of their deity, being sedated and controlled by all its folkloric splendor, while I, with every pound of heaved earth, positioned my conscience and understanding above the masses. The deeper down I dug, the clearer my vision became.

I got up and resumed the dig. By the time the hole was so deep that only my head was above ground, I knew then that I was above the laws of man and his religions. With the vision to inspire law and dogma, I was ready to cast judgment on Steve Jahl.

Does he live or die? It would be my prerogative.

I climbed out of the hole, leaving the shovel behind and took the can of spray paint, painting the words "Merry Christmas" on Steve's headstone, then proceeded to traverse down the mountain. I got in my van and drove to the Super Store to buy a rope, t-ball bat and duct tape. I placed it on the floorboards between the front seats of my van.

    It was all set. Everything was ready. After work, I would go and wish Steve a happy holiday.

CHAPTER 4

WHEN I GOT home from the mountain, I went directly into my bathroom, reached into the shower and turned it hot, letting my clothes drop to the floor, stepping inside.

"Oh Steve," I said, the steamy water washing away my chill, "you're going to die tonight. They say the idle mind is the devil's tool. Well you've got time to think while moppin' floors. On the job you daydream. In the hall with a mop, in the bathroom with a scrub brush in your hand, Steve, your mind's been very active."

My energy waned. Everything that was keeping me alive seemed to be rushing down like the spray from the showerhead.

I've got to kill that son of a bitch, I thought, losing the will to stand. I coughed out a barrage of water, pushing my forehead into the shower's tiled wall, spitting out half my lung down the drain. I waited for the phlegm to enter the drainpipe before sitting down, letting the water gush over my head and eyes.

Steve is going to die tonight, after work, when it turns Christmas at midnight. I had to be at my job at five so it would play out nicely.

The water was slowly turning cold so I shut off the shower and got out. I wiped away the steamy condensation to look at my reflection in the mirror. I hadn't shaved in a while. Something about my appearance reminded me of a statue I had once seen as a kid. This event burned an impression into my memory.

My folks once took me to eat at a Guatemalan restaurant where I would stuff myself with tamales covered in guacamole. In the far back corner of the restaurant was a painted hollow ceramic statue, sitting on an ornately carved dark wood chair, under a piñata.

The statue wore a bolero hat with a matching brown jacket and a bolo tie around its collar. Lying on its lap was a bottle of tequila. It had a thick mustache and a cigar that some phantom person had shoved into its mouth.

I stood looking into its glass eyes, captivated, as if I could see something of myself in the statue.

"It's Hermano San Simon," said our waitress, surprising me from behind. She leaned down to hand me a piece of candy. "He is the brother of Simon Peter, the disciple of Our Lord Jesus Christo. Here, give him this candy as an offering."

Her hair was in a bun and she wore a red and blue striped suna dress. I looked at the candy. It was a sugar skull from the *Day of the Dead*.

"Give the statue candy?" I asked.

"Yes. It will bring you good luck and the deed will come back to you. People give it tequila and cigars."

I reluctantly placed the candy in the statues' lap, feeling that the sugar skull was mine.

"It will come back to you," she said, placing her hand on my shoulder.

"Why do people give the statue cigars and candy?" I asked.

"Because he is a god and enjoys the vices of mortals. You can pray to Hermano San Simon and ask him to grant wishes that are so dark and secret, that you would never dare ask Jesus or the Virgin Mary."

"Jesus isn't real," I said. "I don't believe in the bible. It says things that aren't true."
She laughed.
"You may be right, little one, but something out there in this universe is real. And little boys and grown men must do the best they can to understand."

But here I was, ten years later, staring at my reflection through the steam that was causing me to look like the statue of Hermano San Simon. Coughing, I wiped away the condensation with my towel. My appearance had changed. I actually resembled that Guatemalan statue.

Horrified, I turned away from the mirror. "What's happening to me?"

I looked back. It was only my imagination.

After drying off and putting on my robe, I felt exhausted and sat down on my futon couch. Laying my head back in great despair, I began to nod off, dreaming of Steve.

I heard a ring.

"Goddamnit," I said, coughing, trying to find the phone. I'd fallen asleep. It was dark and I dropped the receiver.

"Hello?"

"What the fuck is going on?"

"Who is this?"

"It's Arbo."

Arbo was the grouchy cook at *Ciao Bella*, the Italian restaurant where I worked. They called him Arbo because in his youth, he had been in the habit of drinking Robitussan in large quantities to get high. I don't know if you've ever downed a bottle of that stuff? But if you did, and you lived through it, you'd be so high that you wouldn't be able to say the word, Robitussan. It comes out, "Arbo." So that's why they called him Arbo.

"Your lucky it's slow on Christmas Eve," he said. "You're planning on showing up for work?"

"What time is it?" I lifted myself off the couch.

"Seven. You're two hours late."

"Oh God, I must have fallen asleep."

"You don't believe in God so get your ass in here."

I started to cough as if my body was trying to expel my lungs.

"Wow," said Arbo, "you sound bad, maybe you should stay home."

"Thanks man. I feel pretty awful. I think I've got bronchitis."

I hung up, looking about my living room. Everything radiated this fuzzy moonlight halo, with a sort of granular look to it. I waved my hand in front of my face. It blurred and stretched, moving in slow motion. Everything was surreal and I wasn't even high.

I started to cough, as though expelling the vapors of hell through my lungs, and fell back onto the couch.

"Damn, I should have worn a heavier coat."

My plan about killing Steve Jahl at midnight was evaporating before me.

Steve had to die. I had to be strong if I were to take him on, right in his own neighborhood and kill him with my bare hands. The desire to repeatedly crack his skull on the curb without mercy was being muted by my condition.

He had to die, along with the rest of them. They were all guilty. I could take out the whole family in a midnight bloodbath, even Lily. Covered in her parent's blood, I'd teach her the treachery of television. Teach her not to watch TV while people are in need.

"Argh..." I was growling like an animal. Why did I lover her so?

"Oh my," I said out loud, weaving from dizziness. "I'll just lay down for a bit."

Everything went black.

The phone rang again. It was my mother and my apartment was steeped in darkness.

"You don't sound well, sweetie?"

"I think I'm really sick."

"Aren't you coming for Christmas dinner?"

"Yeah, sure. I'll be there."

I was feeling as if time was moving slower and everything seemed to be glazed over.

"We're waiting on you. If you're too sick..."

I looked at the clock, trying to understand its meaning. It was 7 p.m.

"What day is it?"

"It's Christmas."

I lay silent, too stunned to respond. I had been asleep for over 24 hours and had missed my set time to kill Steve Jahl. Then the doorbell rang.

"Look mom, I gotta go, someone's at the door."

I hung up and stood, trying to decide what to do.

"Who is it?"

"Arbo. Merry Christmas."

I opened the door. There he was, standing under a Tennessee ball cap with an unshaven chin.

"Are you ok, Sam?"

"I don't know, Arbo. I feel like I been drinkin' *arbotussun* myself." I couldn't even speak right.

"Ted's out in the car, we're goin' drinking at the Polynesian Room."

"The Polynesian Room? That dive?"

"I know, the place sucks. But Julian just got a job there tending bar and he's makin' 'em strong & cheap."

"Yeah, Julian's pretty gifted with that sort of thing."

"He's even libel to serve a couple of underage kids like you and Ted."

Arbo was six months older than us, and therefore, twenty-one. Such things moved his life into a wholly different world. I was given the responsibility to help choose the President of the United States but not deemed responsible enough to buy liquor. I guess voting's not such a big deal.

I got a good look at Arbo. He'd already put a head start on getting tight.

"So Ted's driving on a suspended?" I said. "No thanks, I'll pass."

Arbo pulled out a pack of smokes and hit the bottom, so as to push out a stick.

"Well I would've drove," said Arbo, putting the cigarette to his mouth, stumbling as he stood, "but they got my ignition hooked up to one of those breathalyzers and the damn car won't start. I haven't even gotten to the bar yet and I'm registering .09. We were hoping that you'd drive." The cigarette moved up and down, along with his lips.

"I just don't feel too good, Arbo."

"You lazy bastard." He lit up. "I thought you were bullshitting me to get out of work but you look like you're about to die."

I stared him in the eye and spoke, as if possessed by some spirit from the other realm. "I am dying, Arbo. The man who is Samael Maximon Giltine cannot survive this trial. I must die to be born anew."

CHAPTER 5

I SHUT THE door on Arbo & his drunken ways and began to go through everything in my mind. I was doing my best to ignore the fact that I just might be too sick to pull this thing off.

How many days would I last? I had to survive, had things to do. My body was sweating and shivering and I couldn't remember the last time I had eaten. My life force was slipping away ever so slowly. I have felt worse but never like this. It was strange. I knew I was dying.

I put on my jacket, still smelling of mud and sweat and went out to my van to drive to the hospital. The road was like a ghost trail with a yellow line that weaved about under my van's hull. It was as if I were as drunk as Arbo.

My teeth were chattering and I gripped the shaky wheel with wet palms. The road seemed to fog over and I could see the tall lamps that illuminated the hospital's parking lot, giving all the cars a sepia shade.

I staggered into the emergency room, damp and delirious.

"Can I help you?" asked the woman at check in.

"I ga-damn gonna die."

"Sit down sir."

I fell into the chair.

She was chubby under a blue sweater that collected loose strands of her frizzy hair.

"Do you have health insurance?"

"You kidding?" I raised my eyebrow and dropped my jaw. "I chop lettuce for a living."

"Are you prepared to burden the debt?"

"If you don't see me, I surely am gonna die."

"You're not dying sir." She smirked. "I think you'll be ok. We're having a record week, zero fatalities."

She typed my information as I leaned my head back in agony. It was as if something foreign were invading my body.

"Alright Mr. Giltine," said the intake worker. "Sign right here, then have a seat in waiting. We'll call your name."

I was sitting next to a woman who was praying over her baby. The infant's chest was covered with amulets of saints attached to a chain around his neck. In my feverish state, I leaned over and pointed to the baby's charms.

"You Catholic?"

"Yes." She had fear in her eyes.

"Do you believe those charms protect your child?"

She nodded. "They protect him from the Angel of Death. The Grim Reaper can take any form he chooses-dogs, cats, whatever suits the Lord's needs. They protect my baby."

"What saint is that?" I pointed to the largest of the amulets.

"Saint Nicholas."

"Merry Christmas," I said.

I was upsetting her so I quit asking questions and nodded off, waiting for the doctor. It was a few hours before I was seen. He asked me questions and listened to my lungs.

"How long has this been going on?"

"I don't know."

He pulled his stethoscope out of his ears, began writing a scrip and said, "Pneumonia."

I left the pharmacy, pills in hand and an inhaler in my pocket, thinking maybe I should stop by the Polynesian Room to catch up with Arbo & Ted.

The bar was just down the street from the hospital. It was in this large outdoor mall built in the early fifties, a real piece of work in its day. It was a huge rectangular building plunked in the middle of a massive parking lot that was mostly empty, with its look of old concrete, mildew and asbestos. Through the middle of the mall ran a garbage-lined alley. There was a door back there where underage kids like me could get into the tavern.

The Polynesian Room was the lounge of this seedy Asian restaurant that faced the west side of the mall. The tables mostly sat empty, even at lunch. Nobody wanted their shitty food but came for the booze, especially if Julian was tending bar. This guy was so heavy handed and excessive pouring drinks, he was practically givin' it away.

One sex-on-the-beach from the Polynesian Room and you'd be ready to talk to any girl.

The walls were covered in bamboo paneling and rice paper lamps. Arbo was in the corner booth, next to the bar, holding court. Ted was off somewhere, doing things he probably shouldn't be doing. Some guy was croaking out the *Go-Go's*, "*Head Over Heals*," on the karaoke machine as people ignored him.

"Julian," I said, fighting my way to the bar, "get me a Jägermeister to wash down this here medicine."

"Don't bother showing me your ID, Sam," said Julian. "We all know your not twenty-one."

Julian was wearing a black sort of pirate type shirt, the kind with the frills around a low cut collar. He wore spectacles that gave him this sci-fi nerd, clean cut, John Lennon type look.

I pushed my way over to Arbo's table.

"Sam," hollered Arbo. "What are you doin' out of bed?"

"Just got out of the hospital. I got pneumonia."

Arbo had this young girl with red hair hangin' off his arm.

"Little Red, this is Samael Giltine."

"Pleased to meet you," I said.

"New out here?" she asked, tapping ash off her cigarette into the tray.

"No," said Arbo, "Sam doesn't like to come out to the bar. He's just that way. He's in love with that underage whore, Lilith Jahl."

His words struck a chord, reminding me of what I had to do and how committed I was to seeing it through. I needed to leave this place and kill Steve.

"I got to go, Arbo. I just wanted to say goodbye to you and Ted, in case I don't see you guys again."

"You aren't dying, are you?"

"No. Just say goodbye to Ted for me."

"Yeah, he won't be out for a while. He's probably holding up some stall in the washroom, causing a lineup."

He cackled in an even howl that tapered off into a smoker's wheeze. Arbo had this real distinct laugh, especially when he'd been drinking.

"Go and chase your teenage queen," he said.

"She's eighteen."

"Fuck you, whatever," he said, laughing. "Why don't you just go up to her house and knock on her door?"

"That's exactly what I plan to do," I said with steel resolve. If he only knew, I'd be courting with mal-intent. I left those drunks to the things they do.

The bar was maybe a half a mile from where the Jahls lived so I drove by their house. It was well after midnight and now December 26th. I parked my car about a block away, glancing at the t-ball bat next to my seat. It was new and shined under the streetlamp. I'd knock Steve on the head and bury him alive in the grave I dug up on that mountain.

"I'll put a few dents in that shiny bat tonight," I said.

Slowly picking up the bat, I walked toward their house. The television light blinked, ever changing, throughout the living room window. It was quiet, no dogs or cats. Leafless Russian olive trees lined the sidewalk, providing shadow from the haunting moon as I slowly crept up through their yard.

How should I do this? How could I get Steve out of the house? What if Steve called Dan for help? Dan and Steve combined would surely kick my ass and I'd be imprisoned while they walked free.

I was coming to terms with the fact that I hadn't really thought this through, feeling a little insecure about the thing.

Standing maybe five feet from their front door, I could see inside the living room window. The curtains were so thin they were translucent.

No Steve. Dan and Emily were nowhere in sight, just Lily watching TV in her panties and a t-shirt, all droned out from the glare of the tube. Her legs were so creamy and soft and her blonde locks fell loosely over her skintight cotton shirt. I knelt down and put my face close to the window, peering at her lovingly, caressing every inch of her body with my eyes.

Why did I have to pine for her? I wanted to hate her. The conflicting emotions were bringing my fever to the front of my cerebral cortex.

"Quit being weak," I said. "Focus."

Was Steve even home?

Something caught my attention on the driveway. It was a "For Sale" sign taped to the inside of the driver's window of Steve's Plymouth Duster. He was leaving town!

I moved my attention back to Lily, studying her stout thighs. Years of lusting after her, mingled with guilt and hatred, surrounded me. And here she was, sponged out to the TV, just like she did when her brother was forcing himself on my sister. I imagined her turning up the television volume to drown out Amanda's pleas for help. Never interrupt the viewing pleasures of trash.

I looked up from the blob of mindless flesh, almost lifeless on the couch. Her only redemption was her youth, which would over time, degrade into a resemblance of her mother. I noticed a plastic cast of Jesus nailed to the cross. It was crowning the Christmas tree. Probably made in China by Buddhists.

"Fucking hypocrites," I said.

Where their drive met the side of their house sat a gas can that Dan or Steve had left out, being too lazy to put it away after mowing the lawn. It had been rusting since Fall.

I went for it, transfixed with obsessive fury, popped the cap and proceeded to pour the fuel onto a snow-less patch of grass on their lawn in the shape of an upside down cross.

This'll teach you bastards.

Taking my lighter, I lit the gas. Flames flew up like a rally for the Ku Klux Klan.

Families from up and down the street emerged and stood looking at the southern cross burning in the Jahl's yard as I ran for the bushes.

Emily, Dan and Lily poured out of their front door, watching the flames die down, burning a cross in their lawn. Emily pushed past Dan and Lily. "You call yourselves Christians?" she shouted to the neighbors. "That Giltine girl, Amanda, is a slut. She seduced my boy Steve. He's innocent. Which one of you cowards did this?"

I looked toward the left side of the house, opposite the drive. A cherry of a cigarette, glowing in the night, caught my attention. I could just make out smoke emerging from a dark silhouette. It was Steve.

How long had he been there? Had he seen me spying on his sister from the yard? Did he view me as a predator for stalking Lily? Did he see me light his lawn on fire?

I felt my palm tighten on the hilt of the t-ball bat.

He calmly took a long loving drag off the cigarette. Though I could not see him, I was certain he was staring right at me. He took another drag, his eyes glowing as they peered into my soul from the black.

I inched back, around the fence, into his neighbor's back yard. Crouching down, I heard a growl that froze my blood. A dog jumped at me, barking.

"Shit," I yelled, hitting the brute in the jaw with my bat.

I leapt over the fence and landed in a bush, tearing my cloths and skin. In pain, I started coughing, my lungs full of liquid. Feeling like death, I retreated to the fringe of the neighborhood.

When I got home I went to the bedroom to lay down, forgetting to brush my teeth.

I fell asleep without taking my medicine.

CHAPTER 6

I WOKE UP to a knock on the door. My antibiotics were still in my hand and the inhaler was poking me in the hip, left in my jacket pocket. I got out of bed and answered my front door in the midst of a coughing fit.

It was a middle-aged woman, hair pulled into a half-up-do with bangs off to the side and square frame spectacles. Standing three feet behind her was her teenage daughter. The girl, like her mother, was dressed in black. She had auburn curly hair and wore a skirt that hung just below her knees, revealing two well toned calves, spoiled by splotchy white skin.

To my astonishment, the teenager was holding a baby under a terrycloth towel as it nursed. I wasn't sure if what I was seeing was rooted in reality. Things had become so slippery with my brain since I had been collecting water on my lungs.

"Are you lost?" I asked in a fog.

"My name is Donna Mahlat and this is my daughter Agrat. We are from the Kingdom Hall and just wanted to reach out to our neighbors."

They were Jehovah Witnesses. I stood aghast at the spectacle. The teenage mother looked away in embarrassment, obviously forced into making the rounds as some sort of penance for getting knocked up in high school.

"We wanted to give you a gift," said the mother. "It's a Watchtower magazine and a book of Daniel's prophesies."

She handed me the publications. I took them, open mouthed in a haze of disbelief.

"Thank you. But maybe you might want to convert to Mormonism," I said. "They have the lowest rate of teenage pregnancy in this country."

The woman stared at me blankly. "Thank you," she said, rushing off with her daughter.

"No problem." I watched them depart for the next household.

After closing the door, I felt dizzy and fell to the carpet, succumbing to a deep sleep. I still hadn't taken my medicine and awoke, hours latter, coughing in the middle of the floor. It was dark and I was convinced the pneumonia caused me to dream about teenage dropout girls, nursing their babies while hawking God.

Sitting up, sore from the floor, shivering from fever, my hand hit the book of Daniels prophesies. "Oh no, it wasn't a dream!"

I threw the book against the wall, sending it falling behind the TV set.

"Lunatics," I screamed. "What kind of God sends a teenage slut to my door as a messenger? You all need to burn in hell."

I got up and stumbled through my apartment to my bed. There was my medicine bottle, lying on my sheets. I opened it, spilling pills across my mattress. I crammed a couple of the tablets into my mouth and forced them down dry.

If this girl would have stayed in school and sat through sophomore biology, she would know that religion is bullshit. Man evolved from monkeys. Christianity is a mental disorder. There should be laws against this sort of thing. Steve Jahl's grandfather should have been a eunuch.

My ignorant, bigoted, shouting, turned to delirious mumbling, passing into sleep.

Then a strange phenomenon overcame me that I'll do my best to describe. I felt a presence enter my body and warm me. For a moment, I felt love, compassion, peace and security.

It was as if every second counted for eight hundred years, like a *night of power*. If I had to exist in this moment in time, it would be better than a thousand months. I knew that if I attempted to fly, I could merely will it. But I didn't want to fly. I could experience infinite bliss just by lying in bed and letting the presence warm me.

I felt my life force returning. I dreamed I could see spirits on errands of mercy, like angels, contributing to the ways of the world. One of them approached me and said, "H... M... hummmm."

"Is this the song of the spheres?" I asked in my dream.

Waking, I lay in my bed, pondering my dreams of angels and the warming presence. My condition had greatly improved. For the first few minutes of conscious thought, I considered my recovery to be miraculous and the dreams to be a profound metaphysical encounter. But after a shower and breakfast, I shucked the whole thing off to modern medicine.

I took another pill with a glass of orange juice.

The phone rang. It was Ted.

"Say, I'm a little hung. You wanna meet at the Bucket?"

"Sure."

I could use some coffee if I was going to murder Steve. It was time to return to the task of bringing him to justice. Like a pig, I would drink his blood from a chalice and let it drip from my chin. I got dressed and drove out to meet Ted.

Ted was licking the whip cream off his mocha. "Wow Sam, you don't look so good."

"I don't look good? Ted, your skin looks like fucking concrete. Next thing you know, crystal meth is going to start cutting its way out of your pores."

"I'll take that comment as: you care." Ted looked back to the girls behind the espresso bar. "These chicks sure have got me into coffee. It's an acquired thing. Not a natural thing, like beer or dope."

I took a sip off my latte.

"You know I had a couple Jehovah Witnesses at my door this morning?"

"Don't get me started." Ted sat up in his chair. "They're the only folks alive worse than the Mormons."

"Funny, I told the women she should covert to Mormonism."

"Really?"

We laughed.

"How are the Jehovah Witnesses worse than the Mormons? The Mormons are everywhere. They had this seminary on the campus at Fairdemidland High, remember?"

"Yeah, you're right. How did the Mormons get their own building on the campus of a public school, anyway? Awfully fishy. And don't forget the law," he said. "Every goddamn judge in Fairdemidland is a Mormon. That judge who acquitted the jerk who raped your sister is probably one too."

I needed to change the subject.

"Look Ted, I just wanted to meet you out here to say goodbye. I might be leaving town soon or something. I got these things to do, see."

Ted looked at me with an expression I hadn't seen since we were kids. "Well, I guess you'll do what you must. Have you told Arbo?"

"Shit. No. But I will."

"You should have given him two weeks notice."

"I know. Look Ted, I gotta get goin'. Don't die on me, ok. I'd sure like to see you again."

I got up and drove away in my van, determined to see Steve Jahl. I circled his neighborhood once or twice out of confusion and fear of what I might do. The neighborhood looked peaceful, like a postcard, lines of trees and a thin layer of snow, Fairdemidland gothic.

It was getting dark. I parked and sat, needing to get control of my emotions. It was time to do this thing.

Then I saw him. Steve was carrying a cardboard box to his mother's car. I had stumbled across him moving. The son of a bitch was getting away from me. He'd move to a new town. He was as good as gone.

I began to breathe heavy, my rage taking over my cognitive functions. Emily took her keys and got into the car as Dan stepped out and waved good-bye to Steve who ignored his father. Lily was nowhere in sight.

The car pulled out. I ran toward it, no longer in control. My chest started to ache as I overtook the vehicle, leaping in front of its path. Emily slammed on the brakes and the car slid in the snow, missing me by inches.

"Go ahead, fucking hit me," I screamed. "Hit me. Hit me!"

Emily just sat there turning red. Steve smiled. I looked him in the eye for the very first time and spit on their windshield. "Scum."

They drove around me. I watched the taillight retreat in the distance and fell to my knees in the middle of the snow covered street.

The pain in my heart flourished and erupted from my stomach, seeping up to my chest and neck, causing my face to twitch. I pulled my hair and screamed to the God-vacant sky. Sobbing into the palms of my hands, I choked on the liquid coming up from my lungs in ripping hacks.

I sat there crying until I looked up and saw blue stockings crowned by a red velvet dress.

CHAPTER 7

THROUGH MY TEAR stained vision, I could make out that the girl that stood above me was someone I knew from my past. She wore Converse low tops and a velvet dress that was dime store vintage. She had long black hair and dark skin with Mona Lisa eyes. Her name was Kali Naamah.

I had known Kali a long time ago. Other girl's faces had faded from memory but Kali's came clear out the murky past. It was as if her presence had stepped on my soul, reminding me of how much I had changed.

We once went out on a date but not the normal sort of date. We traveled an hour's drive up to the town of Moses Lake and made out under the moon in the playground of some public school. She knew how to kiss and she felt good under those crazy dresses she used to wear.

It was a wonderful night that I'll remember forever. I never knew where she ended up. And now, here she was, standing over me with an odd stare that left me desperately trying to interpret her thoughts as she looked down, watching me cry.

I dried my tear and hiccupped, looking up at her. If I had believed in God back then, I'd swear she was my twin angel, my spirit guide. But in my limited understanding, I wondered how there could be God when everything was so fucked up: so much death and starvation, power-tripping capitalists trading public welfare for greed? How could there be God when there was Steve Jahl?

That night, I wanted Kali to save me. She was like a benevolent force in the wind, guiding me right. This is what I wanted from Kali as she stood above me, the moonlight washing over me like the sacred manna.

She looked up to the Jahl house. "Come," she said. "You should get out of the street." She knelt down and grabbed my arm, pulling me up. "Why did you do that? Throwing yourself in front of cars is libel to kill you. Besides, if you don't stand up and get out of the snow, you're bound to be sick."

"I'm already sick. I've got pneumonia," I said, coughing.

"I can see that. Is this your car?" She pointed to my van.

"Yes."

"Let me drive you home. I could make you some tea."

"Thanks, I'll be ok."

"I insist."

"Ok. But I'll drive," I said.

Lily's ghost haunted me in the rearview mirror and I wasn't much for small talk.

"I heard about your sister," she said. "Behaving the way you did back there won't earn you your revenge."

"Killing them might," I said, eyes glued to the snowy road.

"Might land you in jail." She smiled. "Do you remember that night you took me out on a date?"

"How could I forget? You were so tender, so sweet. Did you know it was the first and only date that I've ever been on?"

"No. I did not."

"I still feel guilty about calling off our second date."

"Don't," she said. "You were in love with someone else and a complete gentleman. You still love her, don't you, even after what her brother did to your sister?"

"How could I not? You can't control when you love somebody. It imposes a terrible burden on your soul."

"She's a lucky girl to be loved unconditionally."

"Yeah, real lucky," I said, laughing bitterly. "She's a real lucky girl." I pulled the van to a stop. "Here's where I live."

I unlocked the door and let her in.

"Nice place," she said, looking around. "I'm just going to help myself to the kitchen."

"Sure." I sat on my futon, leaning my head back.

"Good thing you've got green tea. Your milk is sour. There's no food in your fridge."

"Kali, you never told me what you were doing out in front of the Jahl's house."

"Visiting my mother. She lives out that way."

"Where do you live now?"

"Out west."

She brought two cups and set them on my coffee table, sitting down beside me. "You know I'm leaving for Seattle tomorrow? You should come with me. It would be nice to have some company. A change would do you good."

"I can't. I have to work tomorrow at *Ciao Bella's*."

"Quit. You can find a better job in Seattle." She lifted her cup, smelling the aroma. "What are you doing in this town anyway? There's no opportunity here."

"I can't leave. There's something I need to do."

"What, carve out vengeance against the Jahl family? You'll only end up in jail. They may have even called the cops over what you did tonight. Anything happens to them and you'd be a prime suspect."

"Are you saying you don't think I have what it takes to pull it off?"

"Good Lord Sam, if you could only hear yourself. You're bent on violence. Think about it. I'm offering you a new start. I doubt Amanda's going to stick around after what's happened to her. The only thing that's holding you here is your mom and Lilith Jahl. You need to get away."

"And who'll take care of my mother?"

"Certainly not you. You can't support her by chopping lettuce and washing dishes. Look, if you're coming with, meet me out in front of the Jahl house tomorrow at noon. If not, I'll see you around sometime."

She stood abruptly and marched out the door. I got up to follow her and quickly glanced down at her teacup, noticing that she hadn't even taken one sip. I ran to the door, but she had disappeared into the night.

"Kali, wait," I shouted. "Stay and finish your tea." It was silent outside. "Kali, don't you want a ride?"

I thought about getting in the van and looking for her but I had no idea which direction she lived.

"Goodbye Kali," I whispered under my breath.

In the dark, I put my head back on the pillow, pondering pitiful thoughts. I didn't want to be a murderer. I wanted to be loved by Lilith and have dinner with her family on Thanksgiving.

But how could I? Kali was right, I was dying in this town.

The next morning I woke at sunrise. I had nothing to do, so I decided to go to the Toad Bucket Café and heal my spirit. I was sitting there, sipping espresso, when this seedy character walked in with a wild look in his eye. He wore a red jacket and had greasy blond hair like an unbathed Irish golem and his presence overtook the whole café.

"Hi" he said, looking about, sitting in the sofa chair next to me. My name's Mani."

I ignored him but he continued to talk.

"Did you know that I went to high school with Roky Erickson and Billy Gibbons?" he said. "Yes sir, back then, Austin Texas had the best goddamned acid in the United States."

Janet walked up, stern in the face.

"Mani, you know you're not allowed in here if you're not going to buy something."

"Aw, come on, Janet. I just wanted to say 'hi' to our friend here. He's got a great aura. He's got this look about him, all peaceful, like an eye of a storm. He's like a son of Christ or a bodhisattva. Did anybody ever tell you that?"

"No," I said.

"Sam comes here to be alone and to think."

"Please, Janet. I've done no harm. I'll be quiet. I need to be around normal people. It helps me control my thoughts."

I could tell that he was stricken with schizophrenia.

"That's ok, Janet. I'll buy him something," I said, feeling sorry for him.

"I'll have a latte, if you don't mind." He began to cough into the sleeve of his sweater. "Thank you. Coffee and cigarettes helps to calm me. I want to be normal but haven't been able to think straight since 1969."

"What happened?" I asked.

"Acid. It was October, the end of the sixties. I was in my parent's basement, lying naked with a girl that I loved. She was so beautiful. We were both sixteen. I was looking at her, stroking her hip when I began to see evil spirits surrounding her. I insisted on walking her home so nothing bad would happen and I could protect her. By the time we got to her house, I had become what I am today."

I didn't know what to say. His presence seemed to bother everyone in the Bucket but me, though he did smell bad. After Janet made him a latte, he started tapping his right temple with his index finger. This seemed to help root his consciousness into our reality and stabilize his thoughts.

"I'm just picken' up your vibes," he said, wiping the foam that gathered around his upper lip on his flannel shirt. "You're like this angel. But you're more like an angel whose about to kill a rabbit."

"How can you be an angel and ready to kill a rabbit?" I said. "Isn't that a contradiction?"

"Have you ever dropped acid?" He came so close to me I could smell his foul odor.

"Once."

"Figures," he said.

I stood up to walk away. "LSD gave me the horrors and I've had flashbacks ever since. I'll stick to Pabst Blue Ribbon, thank you."

"Beer? Shit," he said, following me out to my car. "Alcohol will kill you. It should be outlawed."

"And acid should be legal?" I said, unlocking the door.

"Damn straight. It should be administered to every man, woman and child in the United States of America. If we did, we'd have a utopian society straight out of the pages of Plato's Republic."

"Are you trying to tell me that Plato did acid?"

"Of course not but he probably did peyote buttons or shrooms."

"Peyote buttons? I'm not sure that those types of cactus grew out in ancient Greece." I stepped into my van. "Look, I gotta be goin'."

"Alright," he said. "But I'm just diggin' your vibes. Never seen anything like it. Your aura is like, off the scale. You're a goddamn angel, bro." He observed the look on my face. "You think I'm crazy." He broke into a peel of laughter. "Well I am crazy."

He started to choke on his own laugh. His gaiety dropped and he leaned forward. "Janet called you Sam?" He tilted his whole upper torso back to look at me, as if to take in a different visual perspective.

"Yes, my name is Samael."

"Same name as the Angel of Death. Yes. Yes." Mani leaned forward, letting his jaw drop. He had a mouth of exposed roots and missing teeth. Tilting his head down, he rolled his eyes up to see me and said, "You're an angel but you don't believe in God."

He began laughing uncontrollably, alerting the entire parking lot to his presence.

"Can you buy me some cigarettes?" he said, completely on a new tangent.

"I don't know. I'm thinking of moving, getting out of Fairdemidland. I need to hang on to my money."

"It's just one little pack of smokes."

"Ok." I shut the car door, locking it. "We can go to the 7-11 across the street."

The guy manning the counter saw us coming and shook his head. Mani was obviously a local character.

"Get out of here, Mani," said the clerk.

"That's ok, mac. Sam here's just buying me some smokes."

I threw a ten-dollar bill onto the counter above the lottery tickets. We stepped outside and Mani lit up.

"See that mountain out there?" he pointed.

It was the tallest of a range formed from a large prehistoric lava flow. My father once told me they had an underground control center and bunker that lay deep within the mountain. There, they could control the nuclear reactors and make more plutonium amidst the nuclear onslaught of world war three. He told me that they had missile silos up there as well.

"Yeah," I said, "that mountain out on the nuclear reservation?"

"God lives up there." He blew out grey smoke and pointed west with his cigarette between his fingers.

"I had always wanted to climb that mountain. It's four thousand feet high."

"So you like to climb mountains?" he said, as if reading my thoughts. "I know you do. You should climb it."

"I don't know. It's against the law to go up there."

"Afraid of the CIA?" he said with a cocky grin, blowing smoke around the cigarette that hung from his lip. "Just climb it."

He laughed and patted me on the back, hacking and trying to breathe in between drags.

"I have heard that if you hop the fence and set foot onto the nuclear reservation, it trips some alarm out there and the CIA will emerge out of thin air. Then they send in the black hawk helicopters with armed soldiers to apprehend you. By then, you'll just disappear."

"True, true," he said. "But God will protect you. They say there are no trees up there. But there are trees- trees with spirits. Go climb it and see."

"You're nuts."

"Climb the mountain and find your destiny." He walked off, doing a little dance as he made his way out toward the desert. I got in my van and sat behind the wheel, thinking.

Just do it, I thought. Climb the Mountain. Why not? I always wanted to climb it.

I drove to the westernmost end of Fairdemidland and parked the van at the edge of a vast field. I walked forty-five minutes or more toward the top-secret mountain, until I came across a barbwire fence at the foot of the very steep grade. On the fence hung a yellow sign, written in plain English:

NO TRESPASSING
GOVERNMENT PROPERTY
$10,000 FINE AND FIVE YEARS IMPRISONMENT

"Fuck the government," I said, hopping the fence and mounting the grade.

I pushed up through the desert tundra, nervously watching my back, fearing the CIA. The ground beneath my feat turned to basalt and porous lava formations made my footfall have a millisecond echo.

The echo prompted me to fantasize that I was stepping on the roof of the military's bunker or some nuclear waste dump bubbling within the hollow basalt. But it was just a mammoth layer of uneven porous rock, twisting my ankles to and fro as I tried to walk. The terrain was barren except for the occasional sage that had defied the basalt and grew from its pours.

In the distance I could see a group of bushes that caught my attention. It was accepted fact around Fairdemidland that this was the tallest treeless mountain in the world and to say any different would harm the pride of some jingo Republican who made up a large portion of the male population.

But when I neared those bushes, I found they weren't bushes at all but the tops of trees, covering a small valley-like crevasse, cut from a spring fed stream, giving them the appearance of bushes.

"Mani was right," I said in amazement.

I was ecstatic finding trees thriving on Fairdemidland's goddamn world record treeless mountain of pride. I disappeared under their cover, into the valley, completely out of view of the military or CIA.

"God will take care of you," the old schizophrenic had said. Seems he was right.

Once in the valley, it was as if I were transported into another world. The purity of sound was remarkable, just the soothing trickle of the stream, no cars or planes, no litter or signs of humans.

I sat down to rest and soaked in the surreal scenery of the tree-capped cavern. The trees were thin and curved in the trunk and the grass grew short, giving it the appearance of a well-kept lawn. Sunshine poked through the cover of leaves, conditioning the light and giving off a pleasing shade.

No one would ever know I was there. I traveled under these trees through their valley most of the way up the mountain until the creek disappeared into the hillside spring and the valley ended. I emerged exhausted with the summit in sight. A patch of snow at my feet, I climbed the basalt and made the summit in minutes. On top was a long plain graced by a few odd structures.

The building in front of me was made of white cinder block. *103 Missile Artillery- 2ⁿᵈ Battalion* was painted on the wall in worn plain black font. To the northeast stood a domed building, obviously an astronomical observatory.

Before me was a round iron platform that was slightly elevated and was shaped like one of the fancy custard flans that we served for dessert at *Ciao Bella's*. I stepped onto it, hearing my footfall echo. "Shit," I said aloud. "I probably just alerted them."

I pictured military CIA types wondering what that sound above their heads was. The round metal platform seemed to serve no conceivable purpose until it dawned on me. I was standing on top of a missile silo.

I turned to look down upon Fairdemidland. It looked small enough to grab the whole town and hold it captive within the palm of my hand. With Mount Adams and Rainier mocking me in the distance, I held my arms open wide to channel the power of the sun and take my stance as the god of vigilance, looking after humanity.

"Yes, I am king of the roach and I will do God's job," I shouted to the world below. "Since God's not real, somebody's got to do it. If He won't, then I will. I'm the goddamn Angel of Death."

I opened my eyes and looked to the horizon. In the distance, I saw a black spec, flying right for me. I dropped my arms in panic.

Damn it. A helicopter.

CHAPTER 8

THE HELICOPTER WAS positioned directly over the sprawling field of nuclear reactors that lined the horizon. My zeal sank, knowing I'd been discovered. How could I be so stupid and arrogant to stand atop a missile silo?

I thought about running but there was nowhere to go so I decided to stay put and feign ignorance. As the copter approached, I played the whole thing out in my head. I could just see it now:

"What the hell are you doing out here, kid?"

"I was just hiking, why?"

"Don't you know it's a felony to trespass on a government facility? Didn't you see the yellow sign?"

"Wha... what yellow sign?"

The black speck in the distance grew larger. The closer it got, the less it looked like a helicopter and more like an airplane. With a great thrust, its wings flapped.

It wasn't a plane. It was a giant bird.

I put my hand to my brow to better view it and shield my sight from the sun. It was a bald eagle, with at least a three-foot wingspan. The bird lowered its trajectory, flying right at me, looking me in the eye. It peered into me and for a moment, I could understand it.

Soaring about twenty feet over my head, it seemed to be commanding me to strike. A feeling of surreal lightness came over my emotions, like a bath of clear water, showing me my sole function. I was born into this world to cleanse it.

The eagle cawed. It flew over me and circled back to pass over again. For a moment we were one and I could feel the creature's predator instincts flow through my spirit, filling me with the need to hunt.

I stood, cold from the wind, watching the bird fly away, making me feel like I had woken from a pupal state.

"Go, pursue," I thought I heard it say. Then it flew off, disappearing into the sun.

My time on the mountain had run its course. So I retreated back down the same way I had come. My fate was now tied to Steve. I was the eagle and he was my prey.

Reentering the valley of trees, I pondered the encounter with the eagle. It was similar to the metaphysical experience I had during my bout with pneumonia, like a divine presence washing through me.

"Must be the prescription that I'm on," I said.

When I got back to my van, my legs wobbled out from under me. Fatigued from the climb, I wanted a Grape Slurpee. So when I got back into town, I pulled into the 7-11. There was Mani, sitting on the Southside curb. He smiled when he saw me.

"My friend," he said. "I wonder if you wouldn't mind buying me a cup of coffee?"

He stopped and looked me up and down, his expression changing and becoming quite grim.

"Samael, Angel of Death, did you climb the mountain?"

"Yeah Mani, I made it. Didn't even get caught."

He touched my arm like he was doing an examination.

"You've been in the presence of the Holy Spirit," he said, inspecting me. "The celestial messenger has mirrored you and acted as your twin."

Mani drew close to me. "Do whatever the Holy Ghost has told you. Stay your path."

"I'll do that," I said to Mani, thinking he was full of shit. "How about that cup of coffee?"

When I got home, I immediately went to the fridge, uncapped a beer to wash down my medicine. I sat on the couch, overwhelmed by blood lust, which gave way to thoughts of Lilith.

Lily, oh Lily, I love you so. I want to stroke your heavenly body, gaze lovingly at your procession. We could press against each other, mixing our sweat with your brother's blood. Together, we could destroy galaxies, living in peace, above it all in the fifth heaven.

What was I saying? I was horrified by my own thoughts.

"I don't want to kill anybody," I said, getting off the couch. "And I certainly don't want to go to prison."

My knee hit my coffee table. Kali's unfinished tea was still there, full and unwashed. She would be leaving today and I could go with her.

"I'll do it," I said and proceeded to box up my clothes and belongings.

There was this two-tier shelf that served as a stand for my television. I pulled it away from the wall, exposing the forgotten book of Daniel's prophesies. In a fury, I began reading the book, as if it contained all the answers but the pages were blurry. My head swam. I felt as if I could sleep for a thousand years. And if I did, would the things that trouble me still be there when I awoke?

"Oh my," I said, falling to the floor, letting out a sigh.

Lying on the carpet, sleep overtook me until morning.

Stiff from the worn out padding under the carpet, I awoke on the floor with the Jehovah Witness book still in my hand. I had to leave, abandon everything before I destroyed myself. Determined to take Kali Naamah up on her offer, I began to pack up the contents of my bachelor apartment.

The first thing I packed was the book of Daniel's prophecies. Then I went to my kitchen and dug the Watchtower Magazine out of my garbage. I packed it carefully, afraid of it, yet too scared to throw it away. I remembered what Ted had said. "You could be like a guardian of the community up in his watchtower."

I only had a few possessions so it went fairly quick. By twenty after nine, my apartment was empty. I had everything I needed in a backpack and a switchblade knife that I had inherited from my grandpap in my pocket. I would just disappear.

At an hour before noon, I walked into the kitchen at *Ciao Bella's*. There was Arbo, all hung over, slaving at the stove just to earn enough money to buy a shot of whiskey. I stood under the grease vents, hands behind my back, watching him cook.

"Arbo," I said, lamenting every word. "I gotta go. It's just how it is, man. I won't be chopping lettuce for you after tonight."

"Goddamn it," he said, tearing open the kitchen's cold locker and cracking the seal on an aluminum can of Papts Blue Ribbon. "Look what they've got me drinking when I should be across the street sippin' on some whiskey. I was in a good mood until you got here."

"Well I'm sorry Arbo. I should've given you two weeks notice but I've got to go."

"Don't be sorry," he said, stopping to take a swig of Papts. "Fairdemidland sucks. Get the fuck out and leave while you can. We don't need you anyway."

It was true; Fairdemidland had a way of trapping people. You could leave but you were never really done. I thought about this as Arbo poured a half can of Papts down his throat. "Take a swig, feel my pain." He held out the can.

"No thanks. If you don't need me, Arbo, I'd like to just get going."

"Fuck you. Get the fuck out of the kitchen."

I turned to leave.

"Oh and Sam," he tossed the can into a bin. "Good luck. And don't look back."

"Thanks Arbo, I won't. Don't want to turn into a pillar of salt. And thanks for the job. Sorry I was a fuck off."

"Whatever man. Keep in touch, will ya?"

"Sure," I said, walking out of the kitchen, my head drooping low. I didn't like leaving Arbo like this but it wouldn't kill him to chop his own damn lettuce.

I got into my van and drove across town to say goodbye to my mom and store some stuff in her garage. I sat in front of her house, dreading saying goodbye.

What would I tell her? What was my reason for going in the first place? That I was possessed with murderous thoughts? I just couldn't face her. So I drove off, giving my bed and futon to the Goodwill. The TV and CDs were sold to a pawnbroker who thought I had stolen them to buy drugs.

It was noon sharp when I pulled up to Steve Jahl's house. I could feel the hilt of the switchblade poking my hip through my pocket. I fiddled with it, repositioning it, feeling it and loving its touch.

CHAPTER 9

STARING AT THE Jahl house produced a stunning array of emotions in me. Love, hate, like Cain and Abel, feeling the maelstrom of good and evil that embodies each galaxy in every dimensions. For the first time, I noticed their house was grey. I was leaving town, leaving the woman I loved, and most of al, abandoning my self-destructive need for revenge.

It was the only answer. I needed to get healthy by getting as far away from the Jahls as possible. They were ruining me. I closed my eyes, resting my head on the steering wheel, when I was alerted to the passenger side door opening. It was Kali. She was right on time.

"Ready to go?" She said, getting in.

"Yes." I started the engine.

"You are about to embark on a long journey." Kali smiled. "Seattle is only the beginning."

"Goodbye Lilith," I said under my breath, leaving her house a speck in my rearview mirror.

My van rolled along the bridge over the Yakima River, leaving Fairdemidland in a trail of exhaust. Before me was the road through the nuclear reservation, a panoramic view of weeds and desert, with giant hills of basalt poking through the horizon. A sense of driving purpose rushed through me, as if I were making my way towards destiny.

The large mountain with the missile silos loomed on the horizon to our left.

"Have you ever seen a bald eagle?" Kali asked the question as if she knew the answer.

I thought about my climb up the mountain and how the eagle had flown over me, filling me with purpose and inspiration.

"Yes," I said.

"Did it look at you?"

"Yeah, it flew over me twice."

She nodded and smiled in affirmation. "I can tell. Did you know that eagles are the only creatures who can look directly into the sun and see God?"

"No, I didn't know that."

"The eagle is a remorseless predator, yet it can look directly into the eyes of God. So why then, would it look at you?"

"I don't know."

"The eagle looked at you because it can see that you are its brother. He identifies with you."

"How's that?"

"It knew that if you left all your mortal attachments to fly alone, you would rise above everyone and everything to hunt for what you seek. And if you strike, you will kill. And after you've freed your prey from its living hell, like the eagle, you too will see the face of God."

"I'm sorry, I just don't believe in God," I said, minding the road.

"In time, you will."

I looked at her and tried hard not to convey, in my expression or manner, that I thought she was full of shit.

The road wound down a hill toward a bridge called Vernita that crossed the Columbia River.

"We're a long way from anywhere out here," I said, looking about.

"You are always close to somewhere," she said in a deep resonant voice. "Pull over."

"Why?"

"Pull over. I want to get out? This is where I live."

"What are you talking about?"

"See this gravel road? If you follow it down about a half mile, you'll find a little town called Midway. That's where I live."

My eyes followed a dirt road cutting through the endless sea of sagebrush. "Never heard of it."

She pointed to an electrical substation, dispersing electric current from the nuclear power plants. "There it is."

I squinted, just making out a small group of decrepit houses in the distance.

"The town of Midway was built to service that substation." She looked me in the eye. "You've never heard of the town of Midway because all of its people are dead. Its inhabitants are ghosts."

I sat in silence, unsettled by what she'd said, afraid to respond.

She spoke as if in a trance. "The people of the town died from electromagnetic radiation."

"How do you know all this?" I asked.

"Because I am the only one who still lives there."

She was beginning to seem a little crazy. "I thought you were going to Seattle?"

"Don't worry. I'll be there," she said, getting out into the dirty wind and slamming the door.

"Crazy bitch," I said, spraying gravel. "I'll go to Seattle without you."

I passed orchards and apple trucks on this two-lane country road, witnessing nothing and followed by more nothing. The road curved around large mountainous cliffs. It continued on into a gorge, cut into strong rock by a glacier in prehistoric times, an age of lava and ice, dispersed in steam. You could really feel dwarfed by such things. The wind tousled the car.

It was after six by the time I got to Seattle so I could park without plugging the meter. I didn't know where I was going or what I would do. I just wandered around. The air was cool and seemed to carry a perpetual mist. I stared into the eyes of each face that I passed. It was strange, every man, woman, scum and freak, it was as if I could see the secrets of their heart and could predict when they'd die. I could smell them.

I passed the YMCA and examined the filth loitering about in front of assisted housing. I turned the corner and walked under the monorail, spying a two-story burger house that I could enter to get out of the rain. A frumpy girl in a mustard stained uniform greeted me warmly.

"Welcome to McDonalds, can I help you?"

"Just fries," I said and went upstairs where I could keep an eye on the streets below, watching the people go by.

I was their guardian, perched in my watchtower.

In the far corner, at a table, sat an agitated transient with a glazed stare and pock marked face.

"To hell with all of you," he said, swatting invisible phantoms. "You can go your way and I'll go mine."

He was throwing burger wrappers and other packaging around the café. I could tell he was not present and was capable of anything. I stared at him with the eyes of an eagle, looking down at him, smelling the malevolence and hate rising off his skin. My senses were heightened, my hearing and smell, growing more acute.

He looked around the room and noticed a woman with a baby glancing at him.

"What are you lookin' at?" He growled at her.

She quickly turned away, singing to her baby.

I stared at him uninterrupted, unafraid but patient, waiting for him to say something to me. He was oblivious to my presence but jerked and grunted, making others in the restaurant feel uneasy.

After harassing everyone in the room with his burning, yet restrained energy, the tramp finely looked at me, froze and stared into my gaze as if trying to interpret something. Then he got up to leave.

People were relieved. I left my French fries to follow him and stepped out onto the street. But he was nowhere in sight.

Where, where? I thought.

I stopped, closed my eyes and listened:

"I'll be home in an hour…"

"It's going to rain…"

"Danny be a good boy and you'll fetch a treat."

"Fucking cunt…"

I could hear a thousand conversations, raging for miles in the stratosphere. Focus. Hone the thing. There… a single voice. "Help. Leave me alone. Someone help. No."

It came from a nearby alley. I walked toward the sound of the ruckus, rounding the corner into a piss-tainted laneway. There he was, the agitated bum whose trail I had lost, struggling with a woman, trying to get at her purse.

"Help," she screamed.

I ran into the alley to save her.

"Get off that woman, now," I cried.

He looked at me. I stared at the bum calmly and he gazed back, right into my eyes and saw death.

I turned to the woman that he was mugging and couldn't believe my eyes. It was Kali.

CHAPTER 10

THE TRAMP LUNGED at me and I hit him on the side of the head. A stabbing pang shot from my knuckles up to my elbow. He stumbled back, knocking over garbage, and I kicked him in the ribs, shoving him up against the wall.

"You shouldn't mug helpless women," I said, holding him by the collar.

"Fuck you." He turned his face away, thinking I would hit him. "I don't know what you're talking about."

"Liar." I began punching him in the jaw and ribs. "You were mugging my friend."

It was strange, while beating him senseless, I felt normal for the first time in my life and never as calm. My attention stayed with him, yet I seemed to be aware of everything in the alley, except for Kali. I couldn't sense her presence at all.

He reached up and pulled my hair, punching me in the face, bruising my cheek. The pain filled me with joy, as if I were experiencing pleasures of the flesh for the first time.

Jumping aside, I grabbed him by his jacket and shoved him down into the garbage.

"Fuck you," he howled, trying to get away. "I didn't mug nobody. Leave me alone."

We wrestled around and I could smell cheap wine on his breath.

"You're a lying sack of shit," I said, reaching into my pocket for the switchblade.

The knife shot out of its casing with a click and I rammed it into his gut. Energy ran through the blade, up my arm and into my heart. I held him from behind and twisted the knife, savoring the feeling until he wrenched free. The blow to the stomach seemed to unseat his whole essence of being and his movements became otherworldly, frightening me. I'd never seen someone's eyes appear so alive, yet so near death.

He fell to the ground. Instead of standing over him to watch him die, I knelt down, wanting to touch him. He reached for my neck and started to squeeze the life out of me.

"That's it baby," I said through my closing windpipe. "Kill me. Take me with you."

We were now sharing the same moment. It was both terrible and wonderful at the same time. He had a fantastic hold on my neck and I could feel myself weaken. He was dragging me down with him and I loved it. We lay like lovers in heated passion, but instead of procreation, we were enthralled in destruction.

I lay next to him in the refuse, shielded from the view of the street, knowing no one could see us. I lovingly slid the knife into his lungs and blood began emerging from the corners of his mouth. He slowly loosened his grip and I patiently began to breathe.

"You're beautiful," I said, stroking his hair. "Be at peace."

We stared at each other with locked gaze and I bent down to kiss his bloody lips as he took his last breath. I sat up, enjoying the escaping orgasmic rush that was pouring through my body.

Afterwards, he was still looking me in the eye with dead sockets, his final moments preserved. Getting up, I could see a look of ease over his entire form, frozen in time.

I stood there, taking a moment to observe him. The energy that had animated his frame had now washed into the serene void, dissipating into everything. He was no longer troubled.

Closing my eyes, I tilted back my head to savor the feeling. My heart was beating, pushing ecstatic chemicals through my brain, elevating me to a higher state.

We were now clean.

When I opened my eyes, he was still staring at me, my face imprinted into the back of his retina.

"What am I doing?" I thought, realizing I had just killed a man and petted his greasy hair.

I wiped his blood off my lips and slowly looked about the alley. No one had seen a thing and Kali had disappeared.

My emotions were as even as still water. I couldn't feel a thing, no remorse, nothing. I was now the eagle, a predator, but yet to see the face of God. Kali was full of shit.

Where is she?

The best course of action was to leave the corpse where it was and walk out of the alley as if nothing had happened. Out on the sidewalk, people were so intent on their own personal drives and cell phones that no one even noticed I had blood on my clothes.

I walked to my van and drove to a park in the Green Lake district where they had a public shower for the homeless. No one was about so I washed off the blood in privacy, enjoying the water hitting my back.

Why didn't I feel remorse? Butchering that bum was like chopping lettuce for Arbo or recalling the memories of someone else.

I didn't have a towel so I put my clothes on over wet skin.

On the way back to my van, I came across a preacher man, standing on the curb, dressed in a black suit, tie and white shirt, holding an open bible despite the misty air. Next to him was a wooden sign that read, "Jesus shall return."

He pointed his finger to heaven as joggers and cyclists passed him by. "I looked," he said, "and there before me was a pale horse and its rider was Death. Repent sinners, for the Dark Angel hath come to cleanse the earth. His entry into this age will sound the Rapture and Jesus shall return."

He saw me and silenced his sermon. I seemed to make him nervous and he practically choked saying, "Friend, have you accepted Christ Almighty as your savior?"

"Never," I growled.

"Without Jesus, you have accepted death."

"I am death."

I decided to return to the site of the killing. A crowd of people had gathered, giving me shelter from accusing eyes.

To my dismay, they had found the body.

CHAPTER 11

"WHAT'S GOING ON?" asked one of the crowd.

"I think it's a homicide," said another.

I listened, sweating and feeling short of breath.

After many minutes, (or was it hours?) two paramedics carried the corpse out on a stretcher, covered in a sheet. There was no place to lie out the body bag in that tight alley. One of the paramedics slightly tilted his end of the stretcher and my victim's foot fell out from under the sheets.

The crowd gasped.

"Did you see that? He was barefoot," said this lady who stood next to me.

The foot almost didn't look real. It had a rubbery appearance and a weird tint to the skin.

"Someone stole his shoes," I said to myself.

The purple tinted foot disturbed every one. I recoiled in horror.

"Who could have done such a thing?" said a man.

I did this? Impossible.

The memories began to flood back, the struggle with the knife, the blood and Kali. What had became of Kali?

No, I didn't really just do this. It was self defense, right?

He was unarmed. You had a knife, I argued with myself.

He was strangling me. He would've killed me.

No, he was drunk, in declining physical condition and twice your age.

What about Kali?

Was Kali even there?

I looked around, feeling that despite my being one of many in a crowd, the expression on my face was branding me guilty. I calmed down, noticing that everyone standing around me shared my look of terror and were transfixed at the horrendous scene before them.

"That poor man," said an elderly woman.

I began the walk to my van, talking to myself.

"That man I killed was hardened and desperate, a soul driven to the edge. He was unable to conform to society's terms," I said, recalling the look of peace that spread over his face in his final moments.

He had welcomed death. You could see it in his eyes. His grip on my neck was just a survival instinct. He wanted to die. I was moving my hands all over the place, explaining these things to myself in a buoyant manner. People were ignoring me, looking away, like I was nuts.

I needed to keep moving and wanted a different place to stay the night so I drove my van into this borough (Georgetown I think it was called) and parked next to an abandoned brewery on a street called Airport Way.

When I got out to explore, my spirit pointed me south. So I walked on the east sidewalk next to the abandoned brewery. Weathered brick, silence and shadows gave the huge structure a haunted feel. The street was empty, save for a moonlit glow and I felt the sudden urge to leave the curb and walk down the center of the road.

The buildings to my right appeared as old as the brewery. You could imagine how the avenue looked back in the 1800s. Nothing had changed but pavement on the roads.

I closed my eyes and saw horse drawn carriages spraying mud through the Seattle rain, as women with high stiff collars and touring hats shied under Victorian parasols. It was as if I had been there in a past life, as if I had lived through the ages.

This place had soul. Poets had lived and died on this road. A neon sign in the distance glowed through the damp night, calling my attention to a greasy spoon and bar called Jules Mae's Saloon. The place smelled of gold rush, lumberjack and all day omelets. I sat at the bar, resting my feet on the brass pipe and ordered a pint of Guinness. Luckily, the barkeep didn't card me.

I looked straight ahead at my reflection, taking a sip of stout in the mirror and noticed a blonde haired woman of about thirty-eight, inviting me to join her with her eyes. I turned and saluted her with my glass. She waved me over.

"Have a seat," she said, scooting over in her booth. "My name's Tamara."

"I'm Sam. Pleased to meet you."

She had short hair, chiseled cheekbones and a healthy body; the type a fellow could lie with on a perpetual basis.

"How old are you, Sam?"

"Twenty-three." I lied.

"I see."

It was obvious she didn't believe me.

"Don't be insulted," she said, snuggling close. "I have a thing for younger men. Would you like to come home with me, Sam?"

An irrational feeling that I was cheating on Lilith Jahl came over me. But the thought of spending the night on the metal floor of my cargo van eased these sentiments.

"Um, sure," I said, thinking of her warm bed.

"I live right down the street," she said, leaving money on the table.

We walked on the western sidewalk, north, back towards my van, Tamara hanging on my arm, wobbling in stiletto heels.

"Do you mind if we walk in the middle of the road," I asked. "I don't know why but I love to walk in the middle of the street."

"Ok." She giggled. "Did you know that during the bubonic plague, people believed the Grim Reaper would walk in the middle of the road?"

I looked down at her.

"This is why people in some countries superstitiously keep to the sidewalk."

"You sure are pretty," I said.

"Thank you. You're pretty handsome yourself."

No one had ever called me handsome, usually the opposite.

"It's funny you should mention the bubonic plague," I said, wanting to change the subject from my looks. "I used to have dreams that I once lived in Medieval Europe, in a past life."

"Yeah?" She smiled, sliding her arm around my waist. "I always believed I was a Russian Princes."

"Maybe you were."

"You never know. Here's where I live. It's sort of an artist commune."

She lived in a corner building next to a set of rail tracks. I could see paintings hung on the walls through the windows.

"An art gallery?"

"Yes. I rent studio space upstairs," she said, unlocking the door. "I'm a painter."

Tamara led me up a narrow winding stairwell, made of old dark creaky wood, dating back to the Victorian Era. An ominous presence began to wash over me and I jumped, startled by a wisp of grey smoke, shooting by my head.

"What was that?" I cried.

The wisp of smoke slowed and I could make out the shady apparition of a beautiful woman, whose appearance reminded me of the fashions of the late 1800s.

"What?" said Tamara.

"I just saw a woman."

"You must be imagining things."

I took a deep breath, slowing my heart rate. I began to see the souls of women in garters and gams, roaming the halls as dusty ghosts.

"What was this place originally?" I said, shaken.

"This building used to be a piano bar and brothel back in the old days."

I followed her down thin hall lined with a dozen numbered doors as the shades of women floated around our heads.

"All these studios were the rooms where the girls worked."

Her bedroom was small and the floor was made from two-inch slats. She lit a candle and I could see various oil paintings of browns and crimson. I took it all in until my eyes landed on a canvas, perched on an easel. The painting spoke to me, as if the portrait were revealing my once and future wife. It was of a naked woman nursing her baby, like the Madonna and the baby Jesus. The picture drew a strong resemblance to that Jehovah Witness girl, who gave me the Watchtower Magazine and nursed her baby on my doorstep. What was her name, Agrat?

Tamara led me in by the hand and shut the door behind us. She looked very smart in a sexy sort of way.

"Do you mind if I have a cigarette?"

"No," I said, nervously glancing at her bed, knowing that she had no intention of making me sleep on the floor.

Tamara slowly breathed out her smoke, as if blowing the vestige hairs on my skin. She pursed her lips to tempt me, previewing what she could offer. "Do you want to make love to me?" she said in a sultry breath.

She was very beautiful but I couldn't escape the feeling that I was being unfaithful to Lilith. My heart sank, wishing I could escape Lily's spell.

Sex is poison, I thought.

My palms started to sweat so I nonchalantly put them in my pockets. There was my knife. Tamara was waiting on my answer.

"I..."

My hand wrapped around the switchblade's hilt.

CHAPTER 12

I LET GO the knife, ripped from my thoughts by a fearsome shot and the overwhelming clash of metal, mixed with the sounds of death, coming from outside.

"What was that?" said Tamara, going to her window and pulling back the curtain. "There's been an accident."

We ran out onto the street and stood looking at the underside of an overturned van, watching its northern wheels spin as papers and shoes rained down upon our heads. A yellow car was crumpled into its front side. I looked over to my right, across the street. A white cloth was spread out like a snow angel, red infusing through it, spreading like cancer, crawling like insects. It was a white dress.

"I think a pedestrian's been hit," I said.

Tamara began to cry. "Oh my God, Oh my God."

I was horrified. Not because people were hurt and dying, but because I felt no remorse. "It is but a symptom of the universe," I said under my breath. "I have felt like this before, in another time, in another form." Maybe I was numb from shock?

"Oh Sam, do something please."

It looked as though a taxicab had collided with it. They were Protestants, on their way home from some religious function. I climbed up onto the side of the overturned van and started helping people out from a broken window. I could hear sirens in the distance.

"There's a woman hurt over there!" yelled someone in the van, pointing to the snow angel on other side of the street.

"I'll deal with her," I said, reaching into the broken window and pulling up a battered young man. "Best thing for you to do, is to let me help you climb out and you can assist these others."

A woman emerged from Tamara's artist commune.

"I saw the whole thing," she said. "Some maniac in the back seat shot the cabby and the taxi veered off and hit this van."

I leapt down, ignoring her and walked over to the bleeding woman. The only way I could tell this was even a woman, was from the blood stained dress. Other than that, her body was indistinguishable and mangled. She was as innocent as she was dead.

Tamara, winced and pushed her face into my chest. Standing beside me, she looked down at the dead woman. "Church folk and a girl crossing the street, it's terrible,"

"Sure is," I said. "Just awful."

The police were looking for witnesses and Tamara went to speak to them. Because of the man I had killed, I avoided their inquiry.

Shaken, Tamara and I returned to her building. Defying the ghosts of many whores, we climbed the haunted stairwell. Tamara stopped, turned to me and affectionately stroked me on the cheek.

"All that business out there has me pretty shaken up." She looked pained. "I really think you're fine but I'm not sure I can make love after seeing that girl mashed up."

"Thank you Tamara. I'm relieved. I feel the same way too."

"You can still stay the night if you want. But I just can't. You understand?"

"I'd like to stay, if you don't mind."

"That'd be nice."

We continued up to her studio, sleeping together, fully clothed, crammed into her small bed.

That night, I dreamt that my spirit was lighter than it'd ever been, even more care free than when I was as a child. I had no burden of flesh or pain of bone. I was walking through a wheat field. The sun was shinning and warmed the shoots of grain that hit my palm as I walked along with my hand out. In my left hand, I held a rusted sickle with a long handle, made from ancient cypress, cut from the town of Lagash.

I made my way toward a massive river that gave life to the region. Workers, indentured in servitude, worked the crops that grew along its banks. They focused on their toil, ignoring my presence.

"Here cometh the reaper," sang their children, working the clay on the banks of the river. "We are not unknown to you but you are only interested in our parents."

"Pestilence spawns the orphan," I said, cutting the grain as I watched their families working. "And wheat makes bread."

I woke from my slumber, in a lucid dream state. I looked about Tamara's room. A ghost of a prostitute stood above me, dressed in nothing but bloody gams. I rubbed my eyes, distrusting my vision.

"Hello Samael," said the ghost. "It's been a long time since you came to me in this room, over a century ago."

"What do you mean, a long time?" I said, so scared I could cry. I was gripped by terror, not from the apparition but fearing my loss of sanity. In defiance, I stood up. "Go away, you aren't real."

"But I am. I lived and worked out of this chamber. "The ghost pointed across the room. "But my bed was larger and sat over on this wall."

My eyes followed the direction that the spirit pointed. There was an easel that held Tamara's painting of the modern Madonna.

"I remember it like it was yesterday," said the ghost. "I had been murdered by a hateful man and was dying. I had started to give my deathbed confessional. You, Samael, were standing over me in your angelic form, just like you're standing over this girl here."

I looked back down to Tamara. She looked peaceful.

"You told me not to worry, that I was safe in the afterlife, for Jesus had married a whore."

"But there is no Jesus," I said, "and ghosts don't exist."

The apparition dissipated and I knelt down to Tamara to get a better look. She seemed odd, like she was no longer breathing. I touched her skin.

She was dead.

"How?" I said in a shaky voice, looking around the room.

There was no sign of anything that could have killed her. It was inexplicable. I ran out of her room, having left fingerprints everywhere. On my way out of the building, I tripped over a newspaper that lay on the ground outside, glancing down at the headline.

Man slain for pocket change and his shoes.

I tore off the rubber band and unrolled the paper. Under the headline was a police sketch of someone who looked just like me.

CHAPTER 13

THE TIMES ARTICLE ran something like this:
    Yesterday morning, a man identified as Carson Big Tree, was found slain in an alley in Belltown with wounds to his chest and stomach. Witnesses claim that Big Tree was seen at the local McDonalds on 6th Ave, behaving erratically.
    Police are looking for a Caucasian male in his twenties with short brown hair, who witnesses claim had followed Big Tree out of the restaurant. Police are currently looking for the subject and are listing him as a person of interest.
    Big Tree was found stripped of all personal belongings, including his shoes.
    My skin bristled like a hunted creature, misunderstood and dangerous. Throwing the paper down, I ran for my van.
    They think I killed that guy for his shoes. The whole town's lookin' for me and now that girl Tamara is dead. They'll probably think I killed her too. People saw me with her last night at the wreck, even the cops. They've got her

name and number. They saw us leave the bar together. What's happening to me?

Looking around, I began to hyperventilate in panic. Everywhere, all eyes were on me. Every shadow knew I was a murderer. Fumbling for my keys, I began to calm, realizing the street was empty.

"Ok," I said, starting my van. "I need a plan. If I stay here, they'll lynch me." There was a freeway onramp a few blocks from where I was parked so I got on and gunned it south on I-5, only stopping for gas. I would drive until got to a place where they didn't recognize me, where my sketch wasn't in the damn paper.

After driving for ten hours, I arrived in Redding California. I didn't sleep much, froze most of the night, staring at the interior of the van until the sun came up. The next morning, groggy as hell, I pulled in to a McDonalds to get one of those breakfasts that's served on a Styrofoam plate. I was eating my rubbery scrambled eggs, when I saw one of the workers wiping tables, looking at me.

The girl had a band-aid on her eyebrow, covering a facial piercing and one of those stupid visors they made their employees wear. She maneuvered her way over to wipe the table next to me.

"You look unhappy," I said.

She let out a sigh. "I am unhappy. This job sucks."

"Must be hard to maintain dignity, making you suit up in that uniform and cover your piercing?"

"Yeah, you've got to leave who you are at the door to work here. Where you headed?"

"Not sure, maybe LA."

Why did I say that? I began to imagine her telling the cops where I was going.

"Wow," she said, "The Sunset Strip. I wish I could go with you. I hate this town. I've always said I'd leave with the first boy who'd take me out of this dump."

"Too bad you're stuck here in Redding," I said, wanting her to get away from me and go back to wiping tables."

She handed her bar towel to a guy behind the counter and stepped outside for a smoke break.

Finishing my eggs, I dumped what was on my tray into the garbage and walked out to my van. There she was, sitting out by the trash bin, smoking a cigarette on her break, her mousey brown hair escaping from the visor.

She kept her eye on me and taking a deep drag, flicked her cigarette halfway across the parking lot and stood to walk toward my van. Paranoid about her intentions, I sat inside, ignoring her. She knocked on the driver's side glass.

I rolled down the window.

"Take me with you," she said.

"I don't think…"

"Take me."

"I can't."

"Your license plate reads Washington ARVB-228. You're going south to Los Angeles, running from the cops. I recognize you from the sketch in the paper. You killed that man in Seattle to steal his shoes. Take me to LA or I'll call the police."

CHAPTER 14

I WAS IMMOBILIZED, couldn't move, think or breathe. She recognized me. What would I do?

"Drive away and I'll walk inside and call the cops," she said again.

My heart raced, my hands sweated on the wheel. "And if I take you?"

"Then I won't tell a soul."

I sat, engine idling, my heart racing, weighing it all out. "You're not afraid of me?" is all I could say.

"I am. If I get into your car, you may kill me down the road. But if I stay here, I'll die for sure. Have you ever lived in a small town where you can't see your future?"

Pictures of Fairdemidland swam through my head. "Yeah, I know what you mean."

"Then take me with you and let me live, really live, even if it's for a little while. I'll pay for gas."

"Get in," I said, stressed.

I watched her sit in the passenger's seat, her uniform looking surreal inside my trashed out automobile. "What about your job? Are you just going to blow them off?"

"McDonalds? Fuck them. Fuck my boyfriend too. He's an asshole." She lifted the sleeve on her shirt, showing a large bruise. "He doesn't mar my face."

I began to get angry. "Any man who hits a woman is a coward."

"What's your name?" she asked.

"Sam."

"Pleased to meet you Sam. My name's Eisheth Percy. Percy is short for Persephone. My grandfather changed it to anglicize it when he immigrated from Greece."

"It's a pleasure to meet you."

We were driving down the road toward the interstate when she tapped on my arm. "Pull in here." She pointed to a rundown trailer park. "I live a few blocks up. I just want run in and get some clothes and a few things. You can come in. My boyfriend's at work. Boy, if he knew I was leaving with you, he'd kill's us both."

"Let him try," I said, nonchalantly.

Eisheth smiled, knowing I'd protect her.

Her house was a dilapidated third wheel with a black POW flag, hanging off the stoop.

"What's this guy's name?" I asked.

She unlocked the door. "Alex. He works at a gas station on the way out of town. Have a seat." She motioned to an old cat piss couch with frayed upholstery, its synthetic fiber poking out of a few holes. "Sorry about the couch. It was the best we could afford on Alex's salary."

She sat down across from me in an old rocker. I was feeling caged in her living room. She deserved better than this.

"I never met anyone who has killed somebody. What was it like?"

"It was self defense."

"And the woman?"

"What are you talking about?" I said, feeling a little uneasy.

"You killed a woman in Seattle too." She tossed the front page toward me in a spiral motion so the headline faced me.

Night of Terror!
Seattle gripped in random serial slayings.

"I didn't kill this woman," I said. "She died in her sleep, I swear."

She looked at me, unsure, then taking a deep breath she said, "I believe you."

I glanced back at the paper. Just below the headline and to the right, was the same police sketch from the Seattle Times.

"Kinda looks like me, doesn't it?" I laughed nervously.

"You're way cuter." Eisheth turned the picture to give it a look. "Yeah, way cuter."

I kept glancing at the paper, trying not to appear too interested in the article, but phrases kept catching my eye, like:

Woman suffocated with a pillow in her sleep.

Witness' at Jules Maes'...

FBI's top profiler, Special Agent Broderick...

"Let's go," I said nervously. "We better hit the road."

Eisheth went into her room and emerged wearing jeans and a pink duffle bag over her shoulder. We got into the van and began to drive.

"Tell me about your boyfriend," I said, minding the road.

"He's an asshole. He works at a gas station on the edge of town."

"What does he look like?"

"Five-nine, blonde hair. Smells like petrol and grease."

"I want to stop for gas," I said.

"What are you going to do to him?" she said, almost exited.

"Smell him."

We pulled into the gas station where Eisheth's boyfriend worked.

"Get in the back and stay low so he doesn't see you," I said.

They pump it for you in Oregon so I got out of the van and waited for him to emerge from the cashier's booth while Eisheth hid in the back. I stood, staring at him, watching his every move. He had overgrown curly blonde hair poking out from under a baseball cap and his thin frame filled his thick flannel shirt like a tent pole.

What's a high-tone dame like Eisheth doing with this hillbilly? I thought.

"How you doing," he said, walking up to the van. "Fill up?"

"Yes please," I said, hands in my pockets, fondling my knife. He popped the cap and started to pump the fuel.

"How dare you keep a woman low?" I said quickly, under the sound of the gas pump.

He twitched with a start. "What'd you say?"

"I said, 'Has business been slow?'"

"Don't know," he said in a western drawl, "just got on shift."

"I've a mind to stab and kill," I said, smiling, my hand on the hilt of my knife.

"What?"

"Would you mind giving it a fill?"

"Oh sure," he laughed, nervously. "You said that before, didn't you?"

I began imagining the smell of his blood, the iron particles tickling my nose as I watched him die. He continued to pump the gas, pretending to ignore me, fidgeting.

Just then, a minivan pulled up to the pump behind us and a small group of children with Down's syndrome poured out of the side door. Their driver and chaperone was a woman who wore medium length hair, blue cotton pants that fit tight over her wide hips and a crucifix that hung between the v of her cashmere sweater, marking her of the Christian persuasion.

"Single file children. You each get one candy bar for the movies."

The kids saw me and became animated with adulation.

"Look, look," they cried, running up to the pump. I stood back in horror. They were drawing unwanted attention.

The kids started pawing me, trying to touch my hair.

"No, no, everyone," said the chaperone in a panic. "Don't touch the man."

She looked at me, turning red, pulling their hands off me. "Step back every one. I'm sorry," she said to me.

"It's ok." I tried to pull free of their groping, my hand still on the knife. They were interrupting my moment with Eisheth's boyfriend.

"Look Ms. Erelim," said one of the kids, "he's an angel."

They all joined in. "An angel, yes an angel."

They touched my arms and face.

"Well at least they like you," said Ms. Erelim, the chaperone.

"He's an angel," said one, touching my hair, "just like that picture of the man in the newspaper."

I could have died.

"No honey, the man in the paper lives in Seattle. And like I told you this morning, that man is a murderer, not an angel."

"But angels can be whatever God wants them to be," said the kid. "They can go inside people and control their bodies, Ms. Erelim. He's got an angel inside of him."

CHAPTER 15

SHIT, I THOUGHT, these kids have recognized me. I looked around, forgetting my disdain for Eisheth's boyfriend, trying to figure out if anyone else had had noticed my resemblance to the police sketch.

The handle clicked and the gas pump stopped.

"Some other time," I said to Eisheth's boyfriend, taking my hand off the knife in my pocket to pay him for the gas.

"Huh?" he said.

"Nothing." I smiled.

Eisheth and I hit the I-5 corridor, going south. Lots of dead towns like Fresno and Lodi, dry of vitality and oppressed by heat in the summer and bad economy in the winter. She was silent for about an hour but kept looking at me. "You're kind of cute."

"I'm not sure I can take anymore of this boring scenery," I said, ignoring her remark and changing the subject by making small talk. "I swear it dulls my senses."

A silence grew between us and I could tell she was considering her rash actions now that she was on the road with me.

"So," she said, slowly and carefully, "you never told me what it was like killing that man in Seattle?"

"You don't want to know." I kept my eyes to the highway.

"Did you really steal his shoes?"

"No. Someone must have found his body and taken them."

"Why did you kill him?"

"He was mugging a woman."

Eisheth seemed disappointed.

"But I don't know if that's the only reason I killed him. My remorse over the thing has clouded my reason."

"And the woman? They said you suffocated her?"

"I told you, I didn't... I don't remember killing her."

This answer seemed to make her uncomfortable, surely causing her to imagine my hands around her neck in a fit of psychotic amnesia.

"So you'll stay in LA?" she asked.

"I don't know. I got family up in the hills just a little north of Tehachapi but I probably shouldn't go, too much to explain. Los Angeles might be a big enough place where I could settle in and no one would notice me."

"Why don't you just hand yourself in? I've read that they don't have much evidence about that woman in Georgetown. And the bum was an accident wasn't it? You were defending that lady. He was mugging her. Maybe she'll come forward?"

"She hasn't yet."

I was beginning to wonder if Kali even existed at all.

"Besides," I said, "I'm not really innocent. As I stood there, over him, sharing his dying moments, I felt destiny rushing through my veins. It was like I was singled out to do this."

I glanced over at Eisheth. She looked much nicer without her junk food uniform and her pierced eyebrow was becoming. "I'm like you," I said. "I could go back home, but go back to what? There's nothing for me there."

We stopped at a truck stop south of Bakersfield and bought lunch and a paper. I wanted to see if the killings were in the news this far south.

"Here," I said, splitting the newspaper. "Help me look. I have to outrun that police sketch."

To my satisfaction, it seemed the story was relegated to the Pacific Northwest.

"Find anything?"

"No," said Eisheth. "The hot story down here is this chemical that they've been using to spray the crops, called Malathion."

I turned away to people-watch, totally uninterested.

"They started spraying at night in Los Angeles to control the mosquitoes," she rambled on. "Seems the hippies and environmentalists are opposed to the spraying. They claim that it harms living things. Seems they had some misfortune with it in Pakistan sometime in the 1970's."

"Sounds weird," I said into my palm, supporting my head with my hand.

"You know, people who spray shit into the environment piss me off." She folded the paper and took a bite of her fries.

I looked out the restaurant window, ignoring her; not caring if acid fell from the sky. Nature could take care of itself.

We got back into my van and drove up this steep mountain pass called, *the Grapevine*. Grey smog pushed against the hill as cars and trucks labored up it.

It was the surreal mouth of Los Angeles, sucking in creatures from all over the continent and breathing out those anxious to leave, their spirit diminished with weary dreams, forever changed.

My old engine was loud and hummed hot; making me suspect it was on the verge of throwing a rod. This was hard land, worked by crushed youth and owned by rich Spaniards, robbed from ancient Mexicans and taken again through manifest destiny.

I gripped the wheel and pushed the old girl up the hill, breathing in the smog that poured through the vent. I loosened my grip and wiped my sweaty palms on my pants as I reached the summit, coasting down to Valencia, the beginning of the endless sprawl of Los Angeles.

On and on we drove. It never seemed to end. Through the San Fernando Valley and Hollywood Hills, it was a palm paradise, crowned by a dark brown cloud of toxic atmosphere.

I didn't know where to go so I just drove towards the tall buildings at the center of town, their strange modern spires piercing the brown polluted sky. I parked at the edge of the city center and we walked to the original pueblo settlement of Los Angeles on Olvera Street. We got out and walked towards the bustle of people. It was an outdoor market, looking just like it did when this was part of Mexico.

Eisheth held onto my arm, squeezing through the stalls of cheep goods, cowboy boots, leather whips and marionettes. Stepping on the ancient cobble, fighting our way through crowds of Mexicans and tourists, I knew I had found a place where no one would ever recognize me. Even if the composite sketch had been in the paper or news, nobody would have cared. This was Los Angeles.

"Let's get something to eat," said Eisheth.

Good smells tempted me. "Ok."

We ate *carne asada* and *guacamole* under the shade of tarpaulin roofed *taqueria*. The tables were covered with white ceramic tiles, painted with blue and red designs. The service was fast. I sat across from Eisheth, her presence weighing me down.

"Where are you going to go?" I asked her, cutting my *asada* with a steak knife.

"I'm going with you," she said. "I want to stay."

"Our agreement is that I take you to LA. Where do you want to be dropped off, the Sunset Strip?"

"I've got nowhere to go, Sam. Please. I'll treat you real good."

My heart went out to her. "My life, my situation, has no room for a woman, friendship or family. I'm wanted by the law."

"You'd be less conspicuous with me. I'd complete you."

She was right. Having a woman around made me less suspicious. I was thinking of this until a Mexican shrine in the corner of the *taqueria* distracted me. It reminded me of the altar of *Hermano San Simon* at the Guatemalan restaurant of my youth. But instead of the Spanish don, sat an ornately veiled human skeleton. Various offerings were placed before it.

"Do you see that?" I said, pointing to the skeleton.

"Yeah, kind of creepy."

"It's similar to an altar I saw when I was a boy. What is it?"

A man began to laugh, sitting at a table across from us. He was fat and had a large mole on the side of his round head. Salsa stained his navy blue t-shirt, over which he drew his finger from his face to his belly and then shoulder to shoulder, making a cross, denoting him a Catholic.

"That's *Santa Meurte*," he said, chewing on a *lengua torta*. "Nobody fucks with *Santa Meurte*. She's the Angel of Death."

CHAPTER 16

I SAT CUTTING my steak, chewing the meat, looking at the morbid statue.

"What does it do," I asked the man, "kill people?"

"It takes their souls, *ese*."

I laughed.

"What, you don't believe in the soul, *amigo*?"

"Oh, I don't know."

"You don't believe in God?"

"No." I shook my head and took another bite of my salty steak, washing the chili down with a wax paper cup full of *horchata*.

"Then how do you explain what happens when you die? Where does all that stuff inside you go?"

I took a spoonful of frijoles and bit the tip off a green onion shoot that garnished my small cardboard tray.

"It is true," I conceded, "strange things do occur when someone dies."

"Like what?" His eyes opened wide and he stopped eating, horrified of any potential insight I could shed into the process of dying. I looked at Eisheth. She looked uncomfortable at my speaking of death.

"Well," I said carefully. "Death could best be described as a kind of reaction."

"Yeah? What kind of reaction?" The man took another bite of his *torta*.

"It's got to do with energy, sort of like a dispersal."

"That's what I'm saying." He hit his hand on the tiled table. "That's the soul, man. How do you know this? Ever seen someone die?"

"I have." I took a bite of rice. Eisheth kicked me under the table.

"No shit? Say, what's your name?"

"Sam. This is Eisheth."

"I'm Marco. You live around here?"

"Just got into town. I've come looking for work."

"They're always hiring where I work. You should come by."

"Will I have to shave?"

He laughed. "Hell no. We conduct movie surveys in Hollywood- corner Hollywood Blvd. & Las Palmas. Just stop by and dress nice."

We finished up and stood to leave.

"Good luck man," said Marco. "Oh, and three stalls down is a pharmacy where you can buy a potion that'll protect you from *Santa Meurte*." He let out an uncontrollable laugh.

"Thanks but I'll take my chances," I said, grabbing Eisheth by the arm and leading her out into the crowded stalls.

"What are you doing talking about death like that?" she said. "You'll get caught with that sort of behavior."

"It's nothing," I said, pushing through the people and ducking under piñatas. "You only get caught when you act like you've got something to hide."

I looked up to a sign over the entrance of a stall called the *Millon Peso Farmacia*. "Here's that stall that the guy in the taqueria mentioned carried protection potions."

"Let's go in," said Eisheth.

"You've got to be kidding. You don't actually believe in this stuff?"

"No. But it looks like fun."

I stood looking at wall of glass vials towards the center of the stall. This was about the extent of the pharmacy.

"Look," said Eisheth. "I found it." She held up a small vile with a skeleton holding a large sickle.

"Put it away," I said. "I don't like it."

She replaced the vile.

"What are all these bottles?" I said.

"They contain potions for use in a *Santeria* ritual."

"What's that?" I asked, picking up a bottle.

"*Santeria* is Mexican voodoo."

"What kind of pharmacy is this?" I said, reading the label. "This potion says *Intelligence?*"

"You read it," said Eisheth, laughing. "This potion will make you smarter."

"Yeah right. They've got everything to cure what ails the whole world, right here. Aphrodisiacs, wart cures, potions to make you smarter, increase fertility and the like. It's all bullshit."

I picked up a vial labeled, *Confusion* and opened it up to take a big whiff. It made me sneeze. "Here, have a whiff."

Eisheth sneezed as well. Alarmed, the shopkeep came out from behind his counter. "*Pinche pendejos*. Get out of my shop."

"Fuck off, old man," said Eisheth.

Laughing, we left the pueblo, heading back to my van. I had parked north of the train station on a street called, *Bauchet* but when we got there, the spot where I left my car was vacant.

"Where's the van?" I said, confused.

"Are you sure this is where you parked it?"

"Yes. It was right here."

"Maybe it's on a street that looks like this one?"

"No, I parked it on *Bauchet*, right here, I'm certain."

I began to panic and we walked around the area many times, only to find my empty space, no van.

"Maybe it's been stolen?" Eisheth put her hand on my arm.

I pushed it away, breathing heavy, vexed from the heat.

"And what then?" I said, walking south along *Alameda* St., stumbling off the curb. "We can't report it to the cops. They'll know I'm in Los Angeles."

By the time we had walked past *East First*, we veered off to *Central* Avenue and then south on *Towne* St. The whole place was riddled with garbage. The bums that loitered about all had this green skin, oxidized from body filth and LA pollution.

Young girls, new to puberty, licked their lips, pitching their body, like wares for cash. They stepping out of my way as I stumbled along in confusion, Eisheth trailing behind. Everyone stared at me, freaking me out, causing me to walk faster to my unknown destination.

"I killed a man," I shouted, raving mad, "and I'll do it again."

"Shh, Sam. Please be quiet."

"Ugh!" I stopped and put my head against a brick wall. Eisheth rubbed my back. "It's that damn potion of confusion from that Mexican voodoo shop. I can't think straight."

Out of my mind, I led Eisheth into an alley off of *Eighth* St., called Santee in the *Garment District*. The street was filled with pedestrians and stalls selling clothes right out of the backs of the sweatshops. You couldn't drive a car through there; nobody would even try. I looked around and saw this great polka dot shirt at a stall ran by this fat Italian. The white dots rose from the rich fabric in this heavenly glow that mesmerized my lust for the thing. Salivating over the shirt, I had to have it.

"How much?" I asked.

"Thirteen dollars."

"Sam," said Eisheth, "you're running out of money. What are you doing?"

The Italian took my money. I put on the shirt and pushed through the thick crowds of people that lingered around tables piled high with cheap clothes.

That's when I first saw you.

You were a beam of light, calling me from the distance, grabbing hold of my attention and forever changing my life. How I loved you at first sight. You wore a red, skintight tank top with a black frilly miniskirt, beaming from under that wild mop of blonde hair. You stood tall, hovering above the ocean of shoppers, elevated by a pair of rollerblades that you pushed with creamy muscled thighs.

You skated by me and I turned to follow. You were awesome, waving to a stall keeper as you snatched an orange from his barrel.

"Hey," yelled the produce man.

You turned and giggled. "Fruit from the earth should be free."

I continued to follow you but I'm not sure that you even knew I existed, at least, not yet.

"Sam, where are you going?" I ignored Eisheth, leaving the alley as you skated off into the distance. I followed on foot with Eisheth trailing from behind.

"Sam, stop!" Eisheth ran in front of me. "Who is she? Do you know her?"

"Be quiet," I said.

"Sam, stop. We've been drugged by that voodoo potion. Snap out of it."

"Huh?" I said, watching you disappear as clouds covered the sky.

She shook me.

"Smelling that potion had some adverse effect on us." As she said this, the sky opened, releasing Elysian rain.

Fury poured down in cursing torrents. Buckets fell, punishing humanity and washing the smog from the atmosphere. The Almighty was cleansing its creation.

"Ah, rain," cried Eisheth, ducking under the falling showers.

The drops were large, shooting through our clothes and pelting our skin. It teemed down on our scalps like hard pellets. The pain instantly sobered me.

"We should go back and look for your van."

"Yes you're right." I looked about as water began overwhelming the storm drains.

We waded through water, at least a foot deep, trying to make it back to the pueblo to find my car. My feet sloshed in my shoes, like walking through Jell-O. If we could make it back to where I had parked, we would at least have a chance of finding my van. Shivering and wet, we came upon the intersection.

To my astonishment, my van was there, just as I'd left it. I stood looking at it in disbelief until I realized I was getting drenched from the downpour. Desperate to get shelter, I reached into my soaked pocket.

"Where the hell are my keys? I've never seen so much rain."

"Hurry," said Eisheth. "It hurts."

I pulled my key ring from soaked pockets and unlocked the car. We sat in the front seats, sopping wet, shivering.

"We should change clothes," said Eisheth, wrapping her arms around her lower torso, shivering."

"Yeah. You go first."

She paused in a manor that told me I could watch her change if I wanted. I ignored her body language. She stood, leaning over to avoid hitting her head on her way to the back of the van. I occasionally glanced in the rearview mirror at her blanched flesh as she removed her wet jeans and sat on my sleeping bag, lifting her legs to slide on a dry pair. Her skin did not attract me, for in time, her flesh would die. I found it distasteful. It was her essence that I craved.

A change had come over me. A week ago, I would have mocked the thought of a spirit or essence, but after I killed that man in Seattle and was haunted by visions of phantom hookers, I was beginning to view the concept differently. I felt something inside that bum leave as he died. And when I closed my eyes, I could feel something inside of me, as if a cosmic force had invaded my body.

I remembered that guy in the Mexican restaurant speaking of the soul and how I mocked him. I had to know.

"Eisheth." I went to sit on the wheel hub in the back of the cargo van. "Do you believe in the soul of man?"

"Yes I do. I believe our spirit lives on after we die." She lay down on my sleeping bag. "Who was that girl you followed, the one with the rollerblades? You looked as though you knew her."

"I don't know," I said perplexed. "It was like I knew her. I felt the burning need to speak with her. It must have been that potion. I wouldn't read too much into it."

"You know you can lay with me if you want. I'll treat you real good."

"I know. You're beautiful to me but it's not as simple as that. You're safe sleeping here. Don't worry, our time will come."

It was now quite dark and I sat watching her sleep. I was tired but knew I should move the van to a spot where I could park it for the night. So I got up and sat in the drivers seat, turning the ignition- nothing, completely dead. The carburetor was water logged and there was still at least a foot of water on the ground.

"Shit," I said, foot pumping the gas, hand turning the ignition.

My head dropped onto the steering wheel in defeat. Then the rain stopped. It was a miracle. I looked around in bewilderment. I popped the hood and got out to see. Standing in the flooded street, I watched the clouds blow east and heard a voice off to my right.

"Wow man." someone said. "That storm was like a sign from God."

I turned and there was a guy in his late teens, wearing a rain soaked flannel shirt.

"God, yeah right," I said, shutting the door to my van.

"Don't believe in God, *vato*?"

"No."

"Then maybe you can still find the kindness in your heart to help me?"

"What do you need?" I looked at him skeptically.

"Help pushing my car. It's just over here in this alley. The water flooded the carburetor and I don't want it to get towed."

"Sure," I said, following him into this trashed lane, past an old wooden door.

The alley was empty, barricaded at the far end and there was no car. I quickly turned and saw my exit blocked by four teenagers.

I stepped back a pace and they circled around me.

"Let's make this easy *vato*, out with your wallet."

I reached for my wallet but found the hilt of my knife instead.

CHAPTER 17

I STOOD THERE, lovingly caressing the knife, eyeing each of them. There were four in total. I would have to take them all.

"Out with it mother fucker."

"I don't think so," I said, slowly moving my stare to get a glance at each one. I wanted to know their faces.

They looked at each other nervously.

"I mean it *vato*. We don't want to hurt you. Just give us the money."

"No." I shook my head, a wave of spiritual calm flowing through me. "You'll have to kill me before I give you anything," I said with Bodhisattva grace.

The kid came up and shoved me, scowling, trying to look menacing. But I could see inside them. I could smell the fear on their skin, knowing each of their movements, even before they made them, as if I had been granted a special perception or instinct.

His friends were cheering the kid on so he went to hit me. I pulled back. He missed and I swung my knife, stabbing his throat, right through the jugular.

Before his friends could tell what happened, I pushed the knife into the belly of the kid nearest to my right, pulled it out and whirled around, stabbing my loving blade into the one behind me. Three down.

I turned to my left. The last one standing had his legs spread, arms out slightly, as if to balance. He looked around, confused about what to do. Two of his friends lay on the alley floor in foot deep water, blood gushing from their necks and a third was on his knees, crying, holding his stomach, blood seeping over his arms.

"I'm gonna die, Chindo," he said to his friend.

I looked Chindo in the eye. He was paralyzed with fear and disbelief.

"You'll be ok, Riley," he said.

"No, I need help Chindo. I think Billy and Carlos are dead. I'm bleeding pretty bad."

"Shut up Riley," he said, backing up.

I mirrored his steps, keeping eye contact, holding up the blade that slew his friends, slowly rotating it so he could see both sides. He was breathing heavy and his lower lip, quivered.

"You gotta kill this bastard Chindo. I'm dying. Oh God, Jesus, please forgive my sins."

I slowly walked toward Chindo.

"Look into my eyes," I said, in a soothing voice. "It's better for you if you die. The way you've conducted your life is unacceptable. I'm here to make it all better."

He turned to run, splashing flood water in all directions. I lunged at him with passionate resolve, determined not to let him escape the alley, stabbing the knife into his back.

"How dare you turn from me? Look me in the eye as I redeem you," I said, grabbing his arm.

I pulled the knife out and stabbed him again, tripping him with my right foot. He slid off the blade and fell into the water. I took my shoe and pushed him onto his back with a slight kick, falling on him and pinning him to the ground in the water.

He looked at me, shaking.

"That's it baby. Keep your eyes open," I said, sliding the blade into his stomach, holding his chin in my grip. "I want you to look me in the eye as you die."

I held the sides of his face gently with my hands, trying not to blink or sever our connection until his stare had turned to death. His face shook, causing his lip to quiver with emotion.

"Don't worry," I said, stroking the side of his face, looking into his eyes. "Let it go. Death is beautiful. You'll ruin the look of peace."

I reached around and hugged him, severing our eye contact only to kiss his cheek. "It's ok baby. Let it go. Let it go."

Something was happening to him. I could feel it receding from each cell of his flesh, even his blood. It was that which gave him life, the essence of his being. It was the Father abandoning the Son, leaving the Holy Ghost to escape to where it came. He had a soul. I had surely felt it.

I pulled out the knife, cleaning it in the water and stood to look about the dead and the dying. I had just rid society of four blights, making my body count five. Or had I killed Tamara, making it six? I don't know. Maybe you could tell me when we meet again.

Like a druid, I held my arms to heaven and once again, it started to pour rain, washing me clean. I looked to the sky but I did not see you. I only blinked from the heavy downpour. I left the alley, wet with a slight seepage of blood on my new shirt that would soon be pure from the acid rain.

I took time to look around, making sure there were no witnesses and left the alley. I rounded the corner and practically ran right into a pimp and his girl. They looked right into my eyes.

"What you lookin' at?" said the pimp.

I ran off in the opposite direction of Eisheth and my van. I didn't want to leave her there, but had no choice. I would comeback later, after midnight. So I walked down to Alameda Ave. and waited under a covered bus stop.

It was crowded with urchin and scum, trying to get out of the rain. Two guys in suits stood next to the street filth, looking nervous. I figured that they weren't waiting on the bus but trying to stay dry with the rest.

"This rain's going to wash all the Malathion out of the air," said one of the suits. "That means they'll spray again tonight."

"Fucking hippie," said the other, laughing and shaking his head. "Next you're going to start building a case for the mosquito."

The bus was down the street, spraying water out, leaving a wake, as if it were a powerboat. I got on and overpaid my fare because I didn't have the right change and headed straight to the back; deep in thought about the four boys I had killed.

Hearing a laugh, I looked up. There you were, the roller skating girl from the garment district, looking into my eyes as if you knew everything I had done. You seemed to be high on drugs, though maybe you exist in a permanent state of mystic awareness or something. You just weren't of this world.

Your rollerblades sat by your side on the bus seat. I glanced at the red nail polish on your toes. They were perfect. You didn't care if I was checking you out. You just laughed.

"Where does this bus go?" I asked.

"No where." You laughed at me some more. "You are going no where. You look as though you've committed some terrible crime," you said, amused.

I began to panic, taking in a huge heated breath that seared the lining of my lungs. Did you know? Had you seen the crime? Did I carry a guilty look? I tried to think if I'd left any evidence back in the alley while you cackled uncontrollably.

"Are you a murderer or an angel?" you said, head tilted in a flirtatious manner with a beaming smile that reminded me of Marilyn Monroe.

Hysteria flashed through my brain, blinding me, causing me to instinctively pull the cord. The bus stopped and I jumped up, tearing out of the pressurized back door, kicking water and making my way up the street.

The rain had finally stopped. I screamed out my stress to the sky as the bus drove off in the distance and the sun dramatically set, poking through the black clouds as it disappeared, leaving the area in the black of night.

I had to get back to Eisheth. So I walked west in the cold air toward the skyscrapers that stood off in the distance. Other than these far off lights, it was as if I were the last man on earth.

There was a sound, coming from the east, in the distance. I turned back to see what it was. It was a biplane, spraying something, as if crop dusting.

"Shit, it's spaying Malathion for mosquitoes," I cried out.

I looked around for some shelter. Just fence and wall. I could smell the chemical, like Kool-Aid before you add the sugar. The plane was flying right at me so I started to run, heaving and turning back.

"No, no."

Closer and closer, I could not outrun it.

CHAPTER 18

THE MALATHION FELL from the sky in a thin mist, secreting into the pores of my skin, soaking into my clothes and sticking onto my hair. It had less viscosity than I expected. I watched the plane fly off into the western horizon as I slowed to a walk. It was over.

"Fuck." I kicked a rusted can across the littered street.

The sound of the grinding engine and propeller dissipated off into the distance, obscuring the plane in darkness. The fleece of my arms congealed into sticky clumps.

"Rain, goddamn it, I need a bath" I shouted to the clouds that glowed with the occasional electric flurry. But the rain did not come.

Nearing downtown, I came across an all night gas station, a pod in the middle of an asphalt lot. Awning covered gas pumps surrounded it and an attendant was stationed behind bulletproof glass. You could walk up to his window, speak through the intercom and tell him what you wanted, gum or beer or what have you.

"What do you want?" said the guy, reading a book and avoiding eye contact.

"A bottle of water."

"Arrowhead or Bling?" He was chewing gum with his mouth open.

"Whichever, Mac."

"Arrowhead's cheaper." He walked over to the cooler. "That'll be $2.50."

I put the cash into his metal box and he pulled back on the lever.

"In LA, water's a more precious commodity than coffee or pop," he said.

Taking the bottle out of the metal box, a feeling of hopelessness came over me. I was in this huge city; somewhere I'd never been before, a hunted murderer, covered in poison with nowhere to run.

Disrupted from the experience and not quite myself, I opened the white cap and washed the Malathion off my face. My heart felt like giving away to tears. I was certain this crop dusting had affected me mentally in some adverse way.

"What am I gonna do?" I cried out, depressed and confused, stumbling along, right in the middle of the deserted street.

Formless apparitions flew at me from the depths of my peripheral vision. They were like wisps, haunting hallucinations, disappearing as I turned to look at them. I was spooked by each shadow, scared of the night. Then, the ghosts of the five men I had killed joined the haunts and gremlins. They came to torment me, laughing and following me along.

"Leave me alone," I shouted at the apparitions. "I didn't kill you. You fucking did it to yourselves."

The first man I had killed materialized before me, barefoot, in tattered clothes. Even his ghost appeared sloshed.

"You drunk motherfucker, you would harm an innocent woman just to stay tanked."

He pointed down at my feet. I was wearing his shoes.

"Fuck you!" I screamed, pulling the rotten footwear off and throwing the shoes at him. They passed right through him.

My four alley victims emerged from the ethereal stratum that sits an inch from our skin.

"And you, you pieces of shit," I yelled at the ghosts of the four boys, hovering around me.

I walked straight through the hallucinations.

"All four of you should have gotten jobs instead of taking money from others. This earth is a better place now that you're gone. It's a sham that the law protects you. Stupid fucking cops."

Hyperventilating, I pushed my way through the phantoms only to stumble upon the ghost of Tamara.

"What do you want?" I shouted.

"Only to love you."

"I didn't kill you. Now I'm fucking blamed for it."

"Your very presence brings death and disaster," she said.

Steam was rising up from the asphalt and I made my way past her towards the middle of a lone intersection, walking under the moon. The traffic lights were blinking and I stopped dead in my tracks, blocked by a black panther, right in my path. I rubbed my eyes, not sure if he were real.

"Easy fella."

We stood staring at each other, the animal seemingly sizing me up. He seemed peaceful and unafraid.

I stepped forward and the panther turned as if to lead the way. An odd impression entered my senses. I began to feel that we shared some sort of telepathic connection and I could interpret its thoughts and convert them into a human pattern. I could learn from the panther, to become like an animal, calm, alert and driven. I smelled things I never could smell before, see and hear from the fold.

"Do you believe in God?" I asked the panther with my mind.

He turned and gave me a look. "Yes, but not in the human sense."

It was not as if I could hear him in my head, like the ghosts of my victims, it was more like I felt it.

"Humans, though they are superior in many faculties," said the panther in his telepathic manner, "cannot believe in something whose nature exists in simplicity, yet at the same time, is so vast that it is unfathomable. For you humans, God must think, have responses and feelings. God has no need of such things. God is everything."

"Panther, is there a soul?"

"You of all people should know. You saw the ghosts of those who you freed. You were there when these spirits left the body."

The panther turned to scamper off.

"Come," it said. "I will show you."

A large group of dogs emerged from every direction and circled around me. I followed and soon realized the panther, and pack of dogs, were leading me back to the scene of the execution of the four boys. My shoeless feet were sopping wet and I quickly tore off my socks and left them in the waterlogged street. A lamplight illuminated the mouth of the alley and my van was still parked where I had left it.

There were no signs that anyone had discovered the bodies.

"Come on," said the panther.

I stopped walking and looked at the crime scene with dread.

Then you came out of the alley, your mop of blond hair, glowing under the streetlight. You were wearing the same red tank top and black miniskirt that you wore in the Garment District and the bus.

Spreading your fingers and turning up your palms, you lifted your arms out about a foot from your sides. The dogs left me to circle around you. One of them turned to me and said, "Avatar."

They took turns licking your fingers as you lifted your gaze to heaven.

"She is God," they said, "a glorified personage."

Then you looked down and the dogs and panther dispersed into the night. You walked toward me and said, "Don't be nervous. Be at ease."

"I, I'm ok."

"There are four boys, dead in that alley," you said, as if making small talk.

"Yes, I know."

"No one's called the police. No one knows that they are there."

You looked again to the sky and began to walk away. Turning, you said, "I want you to remember that the pigs are your brothers and Change and Death are siblings, their law rules the universe. Samael, I want you to change, then make love to your sister, Death."

You turned and left me standing in the street. I'm going mad, I thought.

I got into my van. Eisheth stirred, hearing me climb over the drivers seat to get into the back.

"Where did you go? I thought I heard you talking to someone outside and then you disappeared."

"Can you drive? I've been sprayed with Malathion and I think it's affected my thoughts," I said, feeding through a duffle bag for a pair of socks and shoes.

She looked at me with horror. "Are you ok?"

"Yeah. I just want to get out of here."

She got up and sat behind the wheel. "Where are we going?"

"East," I said. "There's factories southeast of here and not very populated. We could probably find somewhere to park for the night."

We drove down a street called Vernon Avenue and parked next to a sausage factory. I could hear pigs snorting on the other side of the walls. I turned to look at Eisheth.

"There's something I have to tell you," I said. She looked horrified. "Back there, at the pueblo, while you were sleeping, I killed four boys."

She sat silent, looking at me.

"They were trying to mug me, wanted my money. What else could I do?"

"Would you kill anyone who tried to hurt me?" she asked, afraid of the answer.

"Yes. Have you been hurt?"

"Yes. Lots. But please don't hurt Alex."

"Ok, I won't. Promise. Who hurt you?"

"A pastor of a church I used to attend with my parents."

"What did he do?"

"Someday I'll tell you. Not now. I just want to sleep."

I lay next to Eisheth on the van's cold floorboards. Fatigue overcame my discomfort, pulling me into a deep sleep. I dreamt of you, on your roller skates, skating through the wind, glowing like a goddess. You skated up to me. I looked to your face but it was no longer young. It was old and wrinkled with wisdom.

"Here," you said, placing a blanket over me. "This will warm you."

"What kind of blanket is this?" I asked. "The fabric has a tingly feeling. It's like I'm being touched by something unnatural and wrong."

"Don't worry Samael," you said, laughing like you did on the bus. "What is unnatural and what is wrong? Can you remember the bubonic plague? Can you remember the children scream? How they suffered so."

I heard a cacophony of kids, screaming as if their limps were being torn from their bodies. I sat up with a start, looking about, startled from my dream.

Eisheth was awake. "What's that sound?" she said.

She followed as I stepped out of the van into the night. I could smell a foul stench that filled me with wine like terror.

"It sounds like humans being slaughtered," said Eisheth. "What is it?"

"Pigs," I said, "being cut up for sausage."

She buried her face into my chest, crying. I pushed her off, walking towards the red brick wall that surrounded the sausage factory like a concentration camp. They were slaughtering the pigs for their bacon, grease for the pan.

The pigs howled, human in their agony, crying out in loss for their children and brothers, shrieking in hysteria. But the butcher was silent, standing tall, unemotional, without judgment, just providing meat so others may live.

"If there is such a thing as a soul, could it be housed in a pig?" I said, caressing the bricks of the wall.

Eisheth stood crying, watching me, afraid. I stood, listening to the invisible cacophony that rose above the bulkhead, wondering what the slaughter looked like on the other side. I could not imagine; nothing; just sounds of death reverberating through the universe.

Was my killing wrong- a crime against humanity or nature? Would the parents of those boys wail like those pigs? Was I similar to the rain, a part of the cleansing function?

I was the dispassionate butcher. Humans were my pigs and this city was their trough.

"Come," I said to Eisheth, pulling her towards the van. "We'll find a new place to park for the night."

She lay on the floorboards and cried as I re-parked the van on the edge of a residential neighborhood. I lay down next to her and snuggled her into my chest with my arm around her. I didn't want her to suffer.

I dosed off, thinking about the soul. If I could know the soul, I would know God.

In my sleep I returned to my dream from before. This time you appeared as a white angel, looking similar to my mother.

"Here," you said, covering me as I slept. "You need a blanket."

"It feels odd and tingly," I told you in the dream, "just like the blanket you gave me before."

"You shall be my angel and servant," you said. "You are now Samael, Angel of Death."

As the dream progressed, the blanket turned into a cocoon, simmering my earthly flesh, transforming me from this monstrous butcher into a beatific angel, with glorious wings like a butterfly, the envy of all insects. But I was not a regular angel. I was a killer.

The cocoon smelled like what? Who knows? It seemed to move around me and have a life of its own.

I could feel the change and welcomed my new angelic self.

Then a flash of light pulled me from my dream. I lay still, watching the ceiling of the hull.

There it was again. It was a cop cruiser, patrolling the neighborhood with its spotlight.

As the flood moved about, residual light crept into the van, surrounding the inside of the hull like an after death halo. Through the light creeping in, I could make out the silhouettes of flying cockroaches, hundreds flittering about the inside of the van.

My hand landed on my chest. I could feel it squish something and realized that I was still within my dream cocoon. It was writhing and tickling. Then it dawned on me. The cocoon that had transformed me into the Angel of Death was a million-forty-two cockroaches encasing me in the dark.

CHAPTER 19

EISHETH SCREAMED. "SAM, there's bugs!"

"Shh." I put my hand over her mouth. "It's the police. Don't worry. The bugs won't hurt you. I am the lord of the roach."

The cruiser pulled up and a flood of light poured in, sending the cockroaches flying in all directions.

We lay still. I could hear the car door open.

"I want to check out this van," said a policeman. I could hear him through the van's metal walls.

"Forget it. We've got a call up in the Flats."

The cruiser pulled out.

"Go back to sleep," I said to Eisheth, stroking her hair.

I fell asleep, dreaming visions of past life reflections with lucid clarity.

The next morning, I awoke, sane and ready to start a new life. We ate breakfast at a two-dollar griddle. The place was real rundown with chipped tile and wore out tables. It was probably pretty swanky back in the day, with its California open kitchen concept. But today, it was a real dump and had to lower its prices to make money off the drunks and bums.

"I feel great," I told Eisheth, taking a bite of toast. "I think the Malathion and the voodoo potion are wearing off."

"That's good. I was beginning to worry."

I looked around. An old transient with a smoke stained beard sat in a daze, stirring his coffee. "I don't know how these places stay in business," I said. "Two-dollars for eggs and toast?"

"Eggs are cheap."

"That's good, 'cause I'm running out of money."

"Remember that guy back in the *taqueria*? He said they were always hiring where he worked. What was it?"

"Movie survies," I said, taking a bite of runny eggs. "It's in Hollywood, just off of *Los Palmas*."

"I always wanted to see Hollywood."

"And now you shall. Let's go after we eat."

I really felt nervous about applying for work so I procrastinated in my job search by walking with Eisheth along the *Walk of Fame*, looking for Peter Lorre's star. We walked west, past the big bra shop and makeup museum and came upon a south street newsstand. I began to peruse, looking down at the LA Times and noticed an article about mosquito spraying:

Environmentalists claim Malathion linked to nervous system malfunction. Manufacturers claim accusations to be unfounded.

"Oh great," I said, picking it up to read the article. "Look at this." Eisheth stood close, reading the paper around my shoulder.

"Hey, you gonna buy that?" said the guy manning the newsstand.

I was about to put it down when I saw a headline that read:

Four teens slain in gangland murder!

"Yeah Mac, I'll take it."

I tossed the jerk fifty cents and walked down the boulevard toward Las Palmas.

"Shit. I made the paper." Eisheth looked concerned. "At least there were no witnesses this time. Could be worse. Seems the cops believe the killings to be the work of Mexican gangs."

Eisheth had a look of disapproval on her face. I could tell that she underestimated the excitement of tagging along with me. "Those four boys were slain in self defense."

"That's what you said about the bum in Seattle."

"Look. This is where I'm going. I'll meet you back here in a half hour."

She pouted and walked down the boulevard. I tucked the newsprint under my arm and made my way into the building to apply for a job. A beautiful woman sitting at a desk, with fake eyelashes and a *Vidal* bob, looked up from a gossip mag, blinking and chewing gum.

"Hello. What can I do for you?"

"I'm here to apply for work."

"Sure, just fill out this form. We're in a bit of a bind. Can you start today?"

"Right now? Ok," I said, sweating the Malathion out of my pores. "I've got nothing else to do."

"Oh... but you'll have to get a collar shirt and tie."

"Uh, sure." This annoyed me.

"There's a little shop around the corner that sells cheap clothes," she said, smacking her gum and pointing with the tip of her pen.

I filled out the app and went out to get the shirt and tie. For the juice in me, I couldn't figure out why you'd need to wear a fucking tie to sit in a call center. Must be some sort of psychological manipulation to keep you subservient or something, figuring that if you dressed up like a grinder's monkey, then you'd probably sell them your soul.

Walking back from buying a shirt, I saw Eisheth sitting on a fire hydrant in front of the movie survey place.

"Did you get the job?"

"Yep."

She looked dejected. "I got a job too."

"What's wrong?" I asked, concerned.

"Oh nothing." She stood up and started walking back towards the van along Hollywood boulevard. "Sam, you wont think less of me if I told you that I got a job stripping?"

"Like I'm one to judge."

She smiled. "Sam, you're the best."

I went back to the movie survey call center and they sat me at a desk with a phone and a list. I was partitioned off from about two dozen other drones, slaving for the wage. I was handed a pad with a script that I was to read from after I had a willing participant ready to take my survey.

"Hello, Mrs. Francesco, my name is Sam Giltine, calling you on behalf of the Motion Picture Academic Research Facility in sunny Hollywood California. We are calling to conduct a survey about the movies and are not trying to sell you anything. If I could just have a moment of your time?"

"Oh, Hollywood?" said the woman. "Yeah, I'd love to."

"Great. First, does you or anyone in your home, work for the motion picture industry?"

She told me that her punk teen works down at the multiplex, taking stubs. This means she doesn't qualify.

"Thank you for your time Mrs. Francesco."

If they were free and clear of involvement with the pictures, then you'd continue.

"Mrs. Archer, have you ever seen the movie Titanic?"

"Oh yes, I just love Leonardo De Caprio."

"Me too. I'm glad you loved it. And Mrs. Archer, I'll let you in on a little secret. They are planning on filming a movie staring Richard Gere that has all the suspense, romance and high tone drama of Titanic but set as a prohibition era musical. If that film were called 'On the Eastside' would you:

> A) Defiantly see the movie.
> B) Might see it.
> C) Probably not.
> Or,
> D) Defiantly not."

"Oh, I guess B or C."
"If that same film were called Chicago would you say:

> A) Defiantly see the movie.
> B) Might see it.
> C) Probably not.
> Or,
> D) Defiantly not."

"Oh, defiantly A."
And this is how it went down for many a movie title. We had that sort of power.

I knew within an hour that this job sucked. But what I didn't know, until about two hours into my workday, was that my boss was a dick who needed to die.

His name was Danny, a bitter failed screenwriter who was never able to secure an option. So he lived a life sustained through bullying the people stationed beneath him.

He was not very nice.
I was called up to his office.
"Giltine," he said, sitting at his desk with a stack of my surveys before him.

He had a round head with a side part that portioned his scalp like the black thread on a basketball.

"Giltine... what is it?" He squinted at the name on the top survey. "Sam?"
"Yes, sir."
"We've got a little problem with your spelling."

"Sorry sir, I'll try to do the thing better."

What he, and most folks I've dealt with in my life didn't know, was that I was dyslexic and had learned to read and spell by memory, not phonetically. So when I use phonics, I spell *"beecaus"* instead of *because* and the like. I have to do math backwards and it makes more sense to read or write from the right side of the page to the left. I guess my brain just works differently.

Anyway, this dickhead went on about my flipping the letters of my terms and locutions.

"You see Giltine," he said, "the Motion Picture Academic Research Facility usually hires people bright enough to spell."

"As I said, sir, I'll try to do better."

"You're looking at me like you think I've got something against you."

I sat there, looking at his round head, wanting to punch it.

"No sir," I said, making eye contact.

"Do you think you're better than me, Giltine?"

"No sir, I know for a fact, that all men bleed the same."

He sat there, silent for a moment, staring at me. "Are you threatening me, Sam Giltine?"

"No sir, just stating a fact that all men bleed the same, just like pigs."

I stood from the chair facing his piece of crap desk. "Now if you excuse me, I'd like to return to my cubical."

He eyed me with disdain as I walked back to the phones, both of us knowing I wasn't long for this job. Maybe he wasn't long for this earth? Bosses who intimidate and bully their employees should be stabbed in the gut.

When I got off work, I stepped out into the California night. The air was thick and sticky. You could almost taste it. Still choked by my tie, I walked south to *Sunset* to meet Eisheth. She stripped at a gentlemen's club called the Zekiel.

"That'll be five bucks," said the doorman.

I paid the cover and entered under the red light. Loud music blared from all sides. Symmetrically placed amongst the cacophony were three brass poles with go-go dancers, writhing through the commons like fleshy cherubim blazing.

Lights flashed. The strobe made the bouncers look like two-faced creatures under a glowing sapphire light. I looked to the pole to my left and there was Eisheth, suspended in my subconscious and veiled in still waters.

After the song, she walked up to some fat fuck and took him back to the VIP Lounge where they did lap dances for twenty bucks a pop. Bored, I sat in front of the center stage.

A song I recognized came over the sound system, *Wheel In The Sky*. I looked up and there you were, lowering yourself to the foundation, dancing to the beat.

You pulsed and writhed to the music, stout legs hugging the center brass. Boots, bra and g-string, nothing else but flesh, held me in awe. I tried to say, "hi" but you ignored me, refusing to look me in the eye. I continued to sit, oblivious to all but your majesty and grace.

"Who are you?" My voice evaporated into the decibels.

When the music stopped, you ascended up your pole, floating out of my sight, leaving me in a room full of people I did not know. I walked past the brass pole to my right and conscious of my surroundings, I left the club in confusion, wondering if what I saw was real or just illusion.

I sat on the curb to wait for Eisheth. In a half hour, she came out the back, looking depressed.

"How was work?" I asked.

"Awful. I feel dirty. Those men are disgusting. Why can't all men be like you?"

"What's so great about me?"

"You're strong. You protect me and you're dangerous. You make life thrilling."

I didn't know what to say so I just kept up in my step.

We approached an intersection. The sign read, "WALK." After my foot left the curb, but before hitting the asphalt, the sign began to blink "DON'T WALK." We continued crossing the street, noticing a cop on a motorbike, watching us from under his helmet.

The don't walk sign went solid as I stepped up onto the opposite curb.

"Hey," said the cop.

He'd gotten off his bike and made his way towards us.

CHAPTER 20

HE WAS A big guy, with a phallic helmet that shone under the streetlamp and jockey boots that were shinny, breeches protruding, exaggerating his frame. He was shaped like cock and balls.

"Yes officer?" I said, fearful of any cop.

"I'm going to need to see both your IDs."

I reached into my back pocket; worried he'd recognize me from some picture hanging on the wall back at precinct. My chest hurt, feeling like I couldn't breathe, a fluttering heart making me weak on my feet.

"Have we done something wrong?"

"Jaywalking is a crime in Los Angeles."

"But we made it across before the light turned."

Eisheth handed him her driver's license.

"Washington State, huh?" He shined his flashlight on the card. "You look like a nice kid in this picture, what happened?"

"What do you mean?"

"You're looking a little unsavory, like you need to shave. How long have you been in California?" he said.

"Not long."

"If you're going to be here more than thirty days, you'll need to change this to a California license." He handed back our cards.

"Do they allow you to enter the cross walk on a flashing 'Don't Walk' in Washington State?" he asked, writing on his pad.

"I wouldn't know."

"Well they don't in California. Ignorance is no excuse for the law." He ripped off the ticket and handed it to me. "The fine for jaywalking is one hundred and twenty dollars."

"120 bucks? I can't afford that." I began to swoon in despair.

"If you can't pay the fine, then you need to take it up with the judge." He handed Eisheth her ticket.

"You're a real asshole," said Eisheth, "a fucking piece of work."

"What did you say?"

"I said you're a real prick."

The cop lifted his hand to slap her and I lunged in front of him to block the blow. He grabbed me by the arm and then brought me down, throwing me into a planter next to the sidewalk. He grabbed my hair and shoved my face into the soil, just long enough to give me the sense of drowning in dirt and then pull me up by the hair to gulp for air.

Smelling the mineral rich soil and tasting its exceptional grains, mingled with the pain of my mashed face, I no longer wanted to kill my boss Danny. Instead, this LAPD officer was feeding me reason to start a cop killing rampage.

He had me by the scalp and with a strong arm shove, "umgf," into the begonias, I became one with the universe.

Up from the soil, I take in air. I am spirit rising.

Thud, face first, back to earth like Mephistopheles descending, I am the butcher of men and pigs.

Up again, I see the light of heaven and am at peace with who I am.

Push my face back into the mangled begonias; I am at peace with what I must do. My function is to cleanse, to slowly flow seamlessly through the fabric of life and remove the imperfections and disruptions within the cosmic ripple.

I must return those who have become derailed back to where they came from, restoring balance to the energy source that animates their frames so that they may live again, born anew, fresh without scars or confusion. Through death, I will transform a fleshy tomb of hate into a spiritual temple of love.

I am, Samael, the Angel of Death.

Pain was moving from my shoulder and neck, down between my ribs, leaving me balanced, at peace, curing me of my hate. It was pain but it did not hurt. I could hear Eisheth, hitting the cop and screaming, but her cries were muffled.

It did not matter. Killing would now be instinct. I had completed my metamorphosis and had become the eagle. But would I gaze into the sun and see the face of God? I would find out tonight.

With a sudden jolt, the cop released my hair, letting my head fall into the planter, leaving me there in liquid form.

"Don't ever fuck with the LAPD, shit face." He turned and punched Eisheth in the mouth, knocking her down. "Have a nice day."

I could hear his words but they did not register and were meaningless. He left us there, lying motionless, as if we were nothing, void, a primal embryo or sac. I existed in this inner haze until I opened my eyes and looked up to see you, my rollerblading, pole dancing, go go avatar of God. You stood over me just to say; "His license plate is DMT-627, you must kill him."

I shut my eyes and you were gone.

"Eisheth," I said, lying on the sidewalk, "are you ok?"

"I'm bleeding. That fucking bastard."

"Don't worry, I'm going to hunt him."

"Good. I hope you kill that son of a bitch."

"God is on our side," I said, getting off the cement to help her up. "He's as good as dead."

We went to the van and sat for a minute in silence.

"Are you up to it?" I asked.

"Up to what?"

"Killing him. I was serious when I said I would hunt him. I am the eagle. When I slay him, I will see the face of God."

She looked scared.

"He deserves to die because of what he did to you. I'm asking if you are up to the retribution."

She closed her eyes and swallowed. "Ok," she said in an almost inaudible whisper.

CHAPTER 21

WE DROVE DOWNTOWN to locate the yard where they parked the squad cars and sat in silence. I glanced at her repeatedly, reading her thoughts and emotions. A part of her was exited, thrilled about what we were doing. Another part of her was scared and guilty. She would be born again. In this life, she was a young soul without experience.

    I waited. It was two in the morning when the bastard finally arrived on his motorcycle. A half hour later, he walked out of the building to his car, marked, DMT-627. He did not see me, or the destruction coming his way.

    Sniffing his essence, I followed him with my eyes to his car, my stare reaching out to touch him and understand his motion.

    We tailed him west. People lined the sidewalks, up to no good. They do this at all times of the night in LA. It's alive and never dies, like Satan humming.

    He led me past *One Wilshire*, down the boulevard, past *Macarthur Park*, its dead gangland grass, paved walks and shanty. He took a right on *Muirfield*, past Los Angeles High School. *Muirfield* was a small street, not very wide, lined with quaint stucco bungalows and palm trees.

Stepping out of his car, he noticed my van as we drove past. I parked up by the high school's fence.

"Do you want to watch?" I asked Eisheth.

"No," she said in a cracked whisper, shaking her head.

I left her in the van, walking down to the policeman's house. His lights were on. I made my way up the driveway that lay on the right side of the house and went round back.

From the middle of his back yard, I watched him in his kitchen making a cold cut sandwich. I moved over to the bushes, standing in darkness, waiting. He took his plate and stepped out onto the back porch and sat down in an aluminum frame lawn chair, with strips of red and white twine forming its back and seat.

He didn't see me standing there. I was in the shadows, an arm's reach of him. Like an apple hanging from a tree, I could just extend my arm out and pluck him. But I left him unaware that his life was hanging off kilter in the universal symmetry.

I watched him slowly eating his sandwich, wanting to let him finish his last meal. We were at peace, both of us savoring the night. I continued to wait, giving him a moment of digestion, wondering about you, God, and coming face to face with who and what I had become.

Then I moved. He turned and looked up.

A flash of recognition shone in his eyes as I stood above him, ramming the blade into his neck.

CHAPTER 22

HE HELD BACK the blood with his hand and looked me in the eye, convulsing in his chair.

"Do you know me?"

"Yes. I'm sorry," he managed to say in a gargled whisper.

"Don't be," I said, pulling him into my arms like a crying child. "What you did, you did because you were not at peace. I am here to put you at ease. My name's Samael."

I pulled his head to my breast and began stroking his hair to comfort him. "Now tell me, what are you feeling?"

"I feel cold," he said, bleeding all over me. "But I can tell that it's going to be all right."

As I hugged him tight, I felt a change in him. His energy, that which gave him life, began to dissipate and hover outside his muscular frame. It was leaving him from his stomach, up through his mouth, as if that was where his spirit was centered. I could tell right away that I was experiencing a soul escaping the body.

If you are calm, and in a sensitive state, you can actually feel the energy, or the soul, vacating the human cells. It was fascinating.

I knew then, that you were real and I was not crazy.

"Return home," I said, pushing my blade into his stomach. I hugged him tight, touching him and feeling him slowly turn into something inanimate. "And when you get to the hereafter, tell God I'm sorry for not believing."

He did not reply but went limp in my arms. I laid him to rest on his back porch, crossing his forearms like an Egyptian mummy. I returned to the van with my clothes covered in his blood. Eisheth sat like she was riveted to her seat, her eyes reflecting the moonlight. I went straight to the back and ripped off my bloody shirt, stuffing it into a plastic shopping bag.

"Did you kill him?"

"I freed his soul," I said, pulling off my pants.

Eisheth began to cry. I ignored her and just drove, moving through the night in contemplation. I took *Muirfield* down to *Pico* and hung a left. On *Central Avenue*, I caught a glimpse of some street urchins warming themselves at a flaming oil drum and parked the car.

"Stay here." Eisheth didn't respond but just continued to cry. I headed toward the flame, my sister in the cleansing right, walking past winos talking in garbled arpeggios. I took my bloody clothes and tossed them into the burning drum.

The derelicts began to grumble and yell. "You got a death wish buddy?"

"Yes I do." I briskly turned to look at them. "I have killed six men and possibly one woman. I'll kill again. He whoever stands in my way, I shall sow their soul into the fabric of time. Any of you ready, just step up and be counted."

They all moved back a pace.

"You," I pointed to a toothless gent, wrinkled from exposure. "I can relieve you of all your worries. Step up and we can unite as lovers. Your soul can pass through me when it exits your body."

He cowered back against the urine stained wall.

"No-not your time? Pity."

I turned to leave. I was smitten with authority from on high and imbued with the power of angels. No one dared accost my backside.

That night, Eisheth and I lay in silence, neither of us sleeping for some time. After I was certain she had dosed off, I let my mind wonder. Sleepy visions of past lives once again entered my slumber.

In the vision, I was walking alone in the Judean desert, remembering the City of Sodom, before it lay under the Dead Sea, until I came upon a hill called *Damardan* where sat a village. I reached the hill's summit just before sunrise.

From the opposite side, I could see you climbing up the hill to meet me, wearing the veil of the cult prostitutes from the Jerusalem Temple. You looked into my eyes and stroked the side of my cheek, the Judean wind tousling a lock of your hair. Then you glanced down to the village with sad eyes.

"Some years back," you said, "people settled here to escape a plague that had set upon Juda. Their efforts were in vain. All of them died."

The first rays of the sun were casting long shadows over the mud huts. You continued. "Years later, a righteous man, Hizqil was his name, implored me to raise these people from the dead. I answered his prayer."

You pointed down to the settlement. "Samael, what's done must not be undone. Please, return the people of the village to their rightful fate."

I held out my arms, pushing my spirit forth. At my feat emerged a thousand and one rats, clawing their way out of the earth like a bubbling geyser, each carrying the poison of my soul. They descended upon the village, infecting and killing them all.

You began to traverse down the opposite side of the hill.

"I love you," I said, causing you to stop and turn back.

"I know." You turned around and kept walking. "I made you that way."

In the morning, I dropped Eisheth at the strip club where she worked. She sat, not getting out.

"Sam, last night I was involved in a murder. I thought it would be thrilling but it's horrible."

"You didn't do the killing. I did."

"But I was an accessory."

"If I'm caught, they'll never know you existed."

"Sam, you've got to quit. It's not right."

"We'll talk about this when you get off. I've got to go. I'm going to be late for work. My boss is going to shit blood over this."

By the time I found parking, I had five minutes to spare. I ploughed through the front doors, past the girl who manned the front desk. When I got to the phones, my boss Danny was waiting.

"Giltine, you're sixty-seven seconds late."

"Well as you can see by the sweat on my brow, I did my best but the traffic on the Harbor was..."

"There are no excuses for tardiness."

"But I'm only a minute late."

"Sixty-seven seconds."

"Ok, but this was the first time."

"Giltine, my daddy always said, 'If you're not early, you're late.' On time is late. And you frequently show up one or two minutes to the hour. If you want to score more than a 'Needs Improvement' on your six-month review, you'll need to come to work early. I expect my people to be at the phones at least fifteen minutes before the start of their shift."

"I'll come whenever you like, as long as I'm paid for it."

"You'll be paid when your shift is scheduled to start. You start early, off the clock, to show us you care about your job by doing a little extra."

"You mean work for free?"

"Well I wouldn't put it like that. Consider it an investment in your future."

"There's not a soul here but you, who makes more than minimum wage. There's no future here."

"Look Giltine, coming in seconds before your shift will only get you fired. I have no choice but to file corrective action. I'll have the form ready for you to sign after you've punched out at the end of your shift."

I sat at the phone and started to dial.

"Hello Mr. Hanson. My name is Samael Giltine of the Motion Picture Academic Research Facility in sunny Hollywood California. How are you?"

"What are you selling?"

"I'm not trying to sell you anything Mr. Hanson."

"What are you calling me for then?"

"We're conducting a movie survey."

"What's the catch?"

"There's no catch, Mr. Hanson. We're merely collecting public opinion information regarding motion pictures."

"What do you guys get out of it?"

"It gives us information on how to market movies. It helps to ensure that you, as the consumer, are given enough information in the film trailer, to make up your mind about which movie you might want to see."

"What do you mean?"

"Have you ever been turned on by a preview and paid thirteen dollars to go and see a movie, only to find out that it wasn't the type of film that you were really into?"

"Uh, yeah," said the guy, "the Lord of the Rings. They cut Tom Bombadil out of the story and the theatre wouldn't even give me my money back."

"Oh my," I said. "That's terrible. Well, we here at the Motion Picture Academic Research Facility would like to collect the information that will ensure this sort of thing doesn't happen to you again. If more folks took my survey and expressed an interest in Tom Bombadil, they probably wouldn't have cut him out of the picture. We also collect information about the types of films you'd like to see made."

"Batman. I think they should make another Batman."

"Ok, Mr. Hanson, I'll write that down. So you'll take my survey?"

"I thought that's what we were doing? Are you shitting me?"

"No, no, sir. I would never shit you. We are taking the survey, right now."

I'd been having a low success rate on this particular day. I was having trouble getting people to agree to take the survey. Folks were hanging up before I could complete my first sentence and Danny was claiming it was all my fault.

"Yes, Mr. Hanson, right now, the survey. Do you or anyone in your family work in the motion picture industry?"

"What do you mean, like a movie star?"

"Well there's that but also behind the scenes stuff or at a movie theatre or video rental place."

"Yeah, my wife, she works at *Celluloid Video*."

He didn't qualify.

"Well thank you for your time Mr. Hanson. That concludes our survey."

"That's it?"

"Yes sir."

"Fuck you." Click.

I hung up the phone.

"Fuck you too."

As I said this, I turned and there was Danny, standing over me.

"Giltine, come with me into my office."

CHAPTER 23

I SAT DOWN across from his desk.

"Giltine," he said. "First off, I was monitoring your calls and there is no excuse for profanity in this establishment. We operate at a higher standard at the Motion Picture Academic Research Facility."

"Sorry sir."

"Not good enough. Second, you lied to the client, making assurances that we are in no position to keep. You promised that man that there would be another Batman."

"I think it's safe to assume that they're going to make another Batman."

"We don't know that, Giltine. What about Tom Bombadil?"

"Sir, I was just trying to get him to participate in our survey."

"By lying to him? Stick to the script Giltine. And even after all that, you lost him in the end and didn't complete the survey."

"He didn't qualify."

"There are other issues, Samael. You insinuated that the client was into pornography."

"Come again?"

"You asked him if he ever got *'turned on'* by watching previews of coming attractions. There is no room for perversion here in this facility."

"Sir, I assure you…"

"There is no defense for this sort of behavior. One more instance of pornographic or sexual content in your discourse with the public and you'll be sent home for the day without pay."

I went back to the phones and began to dial.

"What a prick," I said, under my breath.

The next number I called; the guy was completely compliant and eager to take our survey.

"Mr. Mingus. Do you or anyone in your family work in the motion picture industry?"

"Yeah," said the guy. "My cousin is Glen Dixon."

"Glen Dixon?"

"Yeah, the porn star with the big dick. I gotta tell you, it runs in the family."

"I'm sorry sir, since your cousin works in the movie industry, that excludes you from our survey. Thank you for your time."

I hung up and there was Danny. He'd been monitoring my call on the cordless.

"Giltine, what did I just get done telling you about pornographic content?"

"I didn't say anything. He was the one talking trash."

"Don't argue with me, Giltine. You're going home without compensation for today."

"You mean I'm not getting paid for what I've worked?"

"Exactly."

"But I've been here over three hours?"

"And you haven't logged in one survey."

"You know what?" I said. "Fuck you."

He turned around.

"What did you say?"

"I said, 'fuck you.' "

I stood up and swung, hitting him right in the jaw. Then I tripped him and threw him down.

"You're not a nice man, Danny."

I heard the phone drones clapping as I was waiting for the elevator. Danny was yelling.

"Get back to work before I fire every one of you. Somebody call the police on Samael Giltine."

I entered the elevator and rode it down, feeling high. Out on the streets, I walked west from La Brea on Sunset, watching the buildings down the street disappearing into the smog.

"God, I could use a beer," I said, eyeing a Ralph's supermarket. "If only I were twenty one."

Then it dawned on me.

I asked a whore, pretending to wait on the bus. "What day is it?"

"January 30th."

"Today is my birthday."

"Sorry sweetie," she said, "no freebees."

"That's fine, thank you. Sex is not my thing."

"How old are you, sweetie?"

"20,000 years. Twenty one of those have been spent here on earth, with the exception of 1000 nights that were condensed into one evening, back when I had pneumonia."

She waived me off and I continued on down the street until I saw a restaurant, *Norms*, advertising a five dollar steak. It was five courses for five bucks. You start with salad, dressed with thousand island; bread; soup; and steak; then finish up with tapioca pudding.

I sat at the bar in front of the kitchen. The old gent who sat next to me, looked just like Charles Bukowski. He folded his paper and left. I reached over and unfolded the abandoned newsprint.

There it was, on the front page, "Death of policeman linked to back alley killings."

"Shit," I said out loud, oblivious to the fact I was in public.

I read on:

The fatal stabbing of LAPD officer, Cory Kovich, has been linked to a series of back alley killings that, up until yesterday, authorities were calling the work of a vigilante.

"It's puzzling," said Police Commissioner Cameron. "His pattern is quite random."

According to the LAPD, the killing in Seattle and the four boys in Los Angeles all had a certain perverse motif. Each died from wounds to the stomach and neck. All the victims were 'back alley' types, with the exception of Kovich who died on his back porch, a decorated officer of the law.

"If it weren't for fingerprints, we wouldn't even consider the Back Alley Killer," said Commissioner Cameron. "We're waiting on DNA confirmation."

The murderer was labeled the Back Alley Killer, after media speculation that the killings were vigilante motivated. This theory was put in question in light of the slaying of Officer Kovich.

"The Back Alley Killer is not a vigilante," said Special Agent Broderick of the FBI, who first profiled the killer last month. "Killing serves as a form of intimacy for this person. He is probably a-sexual and religious, most likely attends church. The killing of the officer in California stems from a strong disapprobation of the police."

"A religious person?" I said, the old Norms crowd, ignoring me. "What do they know of the true faith? I know true faith because I have seen the Avatar. I am like the eagle. I have been in the presence of God. I don't need to attend a fucking church."

I didn't like that label, the "Back Alley Killer," either. They were lumping me in with John Wayne Gasey and Ted Bundy. Didn't they understand I was delivering Holy Mandate?

The article continued on another page. There, staring back at me was the original police sketch from the Seattle Times. I paid my bill, tipped the waitress and headed to the restroom. Peeing in the urinal, I held the police sketch up and stared at myself.

"Son of a bitch," I said, zipping up my pants.

After washing my hands, I held up the paper and compared it to my current appearance in the mirror. I was relieved. It looked nothing like me. My hair was growing long and I was farming a beard.

I gave myself one last look in the mirror and noticed a moth flittering about my shoulder. I reached up and grabbed it, its wings flapped in my cupped palm. I squeezed, feeling a part of me die as I held down my melancholy head.

Looking back into the mirror, the comparison between the old me, and the new me, made me happy. But the truth is, the rest of the article really bothered me. I knew I needed to get out of Los Angeles and keep moving.

The minute I picked up Eisheth, I could sense that something was wrong. I could tell by her vibe. My heart beat and I began to yearn for her company in a way that bordered on the compulsive. We drove east. She was shaking.

"Would you like to go for a walk and talk about it?" I said, shooting her quick glances as I drove.

"Ok," she said, looking out the window, as if speaking from a dream.

I pulled over and we walked through about ten blocks of residential neighborhood before we spoke a word.

"You're leaving me, aren't you?"

"Yes. I don't want to, but you're starting to scare me." She made a subtle laugh. "I always said I'd leave Redding with the first boy who'd take me."

She smiled as if it was springtime and the whole world was in front of her. I was envious. All I had to do was close my eyes to see the end of my tunnel, drenched in miserable darkness.

"Samael," she said, "seeing you like this breaks my heart."

"What do you mean?"

"You've let yourself go. You talk crazy talk. What's happened to you?"

I kicked a pop can that sat in the road. "You wouldn't believe me if I told you."

Eisheth tilted her head off to one side, eyebrows raised. "Try me."

"Ok," I said, "I have communed with the spirit of a bald eagle and been in the presence of God."

She stopped walking, giving me a concerned look.

"It's true," I said.

"Oh Jesus, God, help him."

"I gotta tell you, Eisheth, there's no use in praying to Jesus. Jesus was an Avatar of God and that body is now dead- died some two thousand years ago. But God is back and has chosen a new form."

"What does he look like?" She looked as though she would start crying again.

"She," I said. "God is a woman. You could say that Jesus has come back but in the form of a stripper."

Eisheth was silent.

"Samael," she said, after careful consideration, "I enjoy a brass pole between my legs as much as the next girl. In fact it's really great exercise. I've done my share of rubbing my ass on men for money. But let me tell you, there is nothing righteous about stripping. I don't think that if God were to take on human form, He'd do it as a stripper."

"She," I said.

"What?"

"She. You said *he* and God is a *she*. And I've seen her working in your club."

"Which girl is she?"

"The one we saw in the *Garment District*."

Eisheth walked in front of me and blocked my path. "Oh darling." She was stroking the side of my head tenderly. "That girl doesn't dance at my club. I've never seen her."

"Do you know every girl?"

"No. There are dozens."

"There you go. I'm telling you, I saw her."

"Samael," she said stroking my arm. "I have to go. This isn't working for me. This whole killing thing is getting out of hand. But don't worry, I won't tell on you."

"I know," I said but she couldn't hear me.

We were walking south on Euclid Avenue. It was about four in the morning, when a cop car approached. He drove up beside us and got out, pulling out his gun.

"Put your hands onto the car and keep them where I can see them."

We did as we were told. This was it, I thought, they've caught the Back Alley Killer. And then, it started to rain, just like it did on my first night in LA when I killed those four boys.

CHAPTER 24

THE RAIN STARTED to ricochet off the top of the police car.

"Damn," said the cop, looking up at the sky, vexed from the downpour. "Hands on the car where I can see 'em and spread your legs."

The water shot from the sky in large drops, bouncing off the hood of the cruiser as Eisheth and I placed the palms of our hands on it.

"I said spread 'em," he shouted, giving the back of my legs a whack with his billy club.

I could feel the pain searing up the back of my thigh, knowing there'd be a bruise.

"What did we do?" cried Eisheth. I looked at her and couldn't tell if she were crying or it was just raindrops dripping down her cheeks.

"Did I give you permission to talk?" He smacked her with the back of his hand. "What are you doing walking out here at night?"

"We were just going for a romantic walk." Murder was brewing in my heart.

"Well don't let me catch you walking around this late again," he said, as if he owned the street or we'd broken some law.

The policeman began to frisk me. "What's this?" He found the knife.

"It's dangerous in Los Angeles," I said. "You try transferring busses downtown. Besides, the last time I was in Boyle Heights, I got mugged."

He let me up and handed me back the knife. We were getting soaked.

"It's against Metro rules for you to carry a switchblade on public transportation. Leave this at home next time you ride the bus. I should ticket you for a misdemeanor but lucky for you, I want to get out of the rain. You better not carry around one of these. People are libel to think you're the Back Alley Killer."

In a flash, I stabbed the blade into his esophagus.

"Wouldn't want that," I said, reaching into the squad car to unlock the back door.

I took my hand and squeezed the back of his neck, just beneath the skull, guiding him onto the hard plastic seat in the back with a shove. Then I climbed in on top of him, ripping off his shirt to get to his bulletproof vest so I could feel his slowing heart.

"You didn't call in when you stopped us, did you? You just wanted to fuck with us for kicks. That was a mistake."

He blinked up at me.

"Pity for you," I said. "Cause I'm going to get away. You could have been the one to bust me for what I did to your buddy Officer Kovich."

"Y... Y... You..."

He couldn't talk, choking on blood.

"Yeah, I'm the Back Alley Killer. You shouldn't have given me back my knife. Honestly, I couldn't believe that you would be so stupid. Didn't your training teach you not to do such a thing?"

He was coughing and shivering.

"Oh, come here baby. I want to share your final breath." I put my lips up to his and sucked in. His essence went right through me.

Keeping our lips locked, I held it in as long as I could, then blew out his last breath like a hit of marijuana, stabbing my knife into his stomach.

I got out of the back seat, stuffing his legs into the cab and shutting the door. I looked around for Eisheth. She was gone. I wanted to call out but the neighbors would call the police. I had no choice. I had to let her go. She was not my destiny.

"Fuck it," I said to myself. "Don't follow her Sam. Be a man and just walk away." She was leaving anyway.

Because the policeman hadn't called it in, I knew I had a little time before anyone noticed he was missing. So I got into the driver's seat and parked the squad car in the darkest part of the street, then walked south, back to my van in the punishing rain.

I spread my wings, feeling alive. The rain was really coming down and my legs hurt from the billy club. It was on *Lorena St*, when the storm drains began to back up and the waters flooded.

By the time I had got down to *Lorena & Pico*, the street had turned into a river, reflecting light from the street lamps. The flood cut through the palm trees, making *Pico Avenue* look like the Nile. The water emptied around a fork in the road like a great river delta, giving the fenced parking lot the appearance of an island oasis. A Mexican seafood restaurant, that sat center on this island, had this phallic obelisk for a sign that shone like the *Pharos*.

My pants and shoes were soaked and heavy by the time I got to the van. I sat behind the wheel, dripping onto the floorboards, surprised that the car actually started. It was time for me to leave. If I stayed in Los Angeles, I would surely get caught. Things were getting out of hand.

The van seemed to float along as I drove slowly on up to *Soto Street*. I had only driven a few blocks when I saw Eisheth walking, soaking wet.

"Get in," I said, reaching over and rolling down the passenger window. "I'm heading north, I'll take you to back to Redding."

She was shivering and crying.

"I'm going home, to my mother's in Fairdemidland. I'll drop you on the way."

"Sam, I've got nothing to go back to."

"Then come with me."

She didn't reply, just continued to cry and got into the van.

After I climbed the onramp to I-5, the road was clear but the traffic was a little backed up. I wanted to beat the morning rush. The sun hadn't come up yet and my windshield wipers were open to full capacity, overwhelmed by the onslaught.

Traffic started to move once I cleared *the Valley* and the sun came up as I crossed through to *Valencia*. The buckets now seemed like rain and turned to a drizzle as I passed *Pyramid Lake*.

We were out of LA and balled it all the way to Bakersfield.

"I have family up in the mountains outside of Tehachapi," I said. "The town is called *Whiskey Flats*. We can stay the night with them."

"That would be nice," Eisheth said in a way that made me concerned for her well being. She was beginning to sink low.

The road that followed the *Kern River* up the mountain to *Whiskey Flats* made me car sick, kept curving and such. Ravines dropped two feet from the side of the little road and sharp cliffs stood directly to my right. I felt like I would puke.

Eisheth looked out the window to the Kern River. "Pull over here."

"Why?"

"Sam, can we take a walk along the river?"

"Sure," I said, short of breath and sweating from carsickness.

She got out and walked to the edge of the raging stream. "I once read that they have an average of seven drownings a year in this river." She turned and faced the white rapids. "I can't live with myself after being a party to two murders. I want to die. I've got nothing to live for and nothing to go back to. I want to end it now. If you love me, you'll let me go."

I was astonished. "But Eisheth, you've got so much to live for. You're beautiful. You…"

She put her hand up to my mouth.

"Eisheth, I'm sorry I brought you into this."

"No, don't be. I asked to come. In fact I threatened you." She smiled at me. "Sam, it's my time. Let me go."

"Don't think this way. You can start a new life. Don't give up hope."

"Did I ever tell you that I used to go to church?" She picked up a rock and threw it in the water.

"No."

"It was back when I was a kid, before I was cast out."

"Cast out?"

"Yes, cast out of their religion, my school, my home and circle of friends. One night the pastor of my church picked me up and paid me to suck him off. Shortly after, he excommunicated me."

I closed my eyes, hurt by the hypocrisy.

"My father threw me out of the house. The only way I could support myself was by turning tricks. Alex took me in. He stopped me from whoring myself out. Alex beat me up, but it was better than working the streets. This is what I have to return to. At best, I'll be a burger girl."

I held her close to my chest.

"Samael, you are an angel. You're blessed," she said with a tear in her eye. "That is, if you can accept grace from a whore."

"Eisheth, God has returned. Not as Jesus, but as that stripper. If God loves the righteous, he loves the whores even more."

She smiled and rubbed the tears away from her eyes. Then she let herself fall back. I tried to grab her but was too late. She splashed into the water.

"No!" I ran along the rivers edge, but she was swept away into the current. I stood, staring in disbelief, knowing that she was gone and there was nothing I could do.

CHAPTER 25

THE RAPIDS TORE through the valley, the sound deafening my cries. I could not save her. Her corpse was traveling down river faster than I could drive. What could I do, call the cops? I had no alternative but to get into the van and drive to my grandmother's house, squinting from the rising sun.

Distraught, I parked my van by the tree next to her manufactured home. My aunt came outside, puffing like a mad fish.

"Goddamn you Samael Maximon Giltine. Where have you been? You've worried your mother sick. Everyone's given you up for dead."

"Sorry Debbie, I was out soul searching."

"That's Auntie Debbie to you, mister."

On the porch, my grandma was all hunched and crying. "I always said that Samael was a delightful child. Used to call him that... 'Delightful.'"

She was getting quite old and preferred to deny any sort of bad feelings or drama.

"Well, did you find your soul?"

"Yes Aunt Debbie, I did."

"What's a matter with you? Maybe you need to be checked for depression."

"I'm fine. I'm just tired and need to rest for a while."

The next few days, I spent a lot of time drunk on Budweiser, laying on my grandma's couch. I missed Eisheth. It wouldn't be the same without her. Sometimes, I'd sit on grandma's porch, listening to the old woman's gab.

"Delilah says they have cheap apples down in Kernville. You still dating that girl Sandy?"

"Lily? No grandma, she was never my girlfriend. I haven't touched a girl in some time."

"I heard that, Samael," my aunt piped in from the kitchen window. "If you're thinkin' you need some, you better stay away from those girls down at *Sawmill Road*. If I catch you down there, I'm libel to cut it off."

"I won't be worrying none about those girls, they prefer the love of their papa or brothers anyhow." I got up and lifted my arms for a stretch. "It's nice out, I think I'll go for a walk."

"You gonna leave me to do all the dishes?"

"Sorry, I'll do them when I get back."

"You remember what I told you about *Sawmill Road*?" she said as I was leaving.

"Yes Auntie."

"Samael always was delightful," said my grandmother. "That's what I used to call him... 'Delightful.' "

"Shut up," hollered my aunt. "You've been sayin' that all day. If he gets one of them Sawmill girls pregnant, I'm cutting it off."

My ideas about sex were just too complex to explain to my aunt so I just left, looking up to the cosmos, wondering about you and your creation. There were even more stars above Whiskey Flats than in Fairdemidland. There were none at all in LA, too many lights reflecting off the smog.

Down by the lake there were some park benches and a boat launch. I lay down on top of a picnic table and looked up, trying to identify certain constellations. The late spring breeze was cool and it felt good to be alive.

I tilted my head to the right, resting my cheek on the tabletop and dosed off. I began dreaming that I saw a man in white cotton robes wading out of the manmade lake. Strange thing was, his clothes were still dry.

Even from a distance, I could tell that he was from India. He had a beard, long wavy hair, uncut like the Nazirites, and lovely piercing all knowing eyes, just like yours.

"Hello," he said, walking up to me.

"Are you a ghost?" I asked.

"Of course," he said. "You should know. You took my body away from me back in 1969. Don't you remember? You came to me as the Angel of Death. My name was Baba."

I lay still on the park table, horrified. Certain memories flashed like a bulb or a latent strobe.

"Weren't you a holy man," I said, "or a Hindu guru or something?"

"Before I became a God-realized entity, when I was young and needed religion, I was a Parsi, but never a Hindu."

"Baba," I said, sitting up on the picnic table, "what do you mean by God-realized entity?"

Baba smiled. "Every living and inanimate thing is an expression of God. If we as humans can realize this, then we have achieved God-realization and become a glorified personage. Now I don't mean to just accept that we are a divine expression, but we must perceive the divine aspect of who we are. This can be done by assuming a subconscious state and realizing the essence of the Divine Expression that created us."

"Kind of like the Buddha?"

"Precisely. Jesus achieved the same glorified state, as did Krishna. At any one time there are fifty-six humans on this planet who have achieved this state of being. Of these fifty-six God-realized beings, there are five who are considered Perfect Masters or prophets. But only one of them is a rasool."

"What's a rasool?"

"You might call it a messiah," he said, looking over me as I lay on the table. "In India, we call it an Avatar. Some call those who achieve this state, prophets. Some of them have revealed scripture but this hasn't happened for some time. Before you took this body from me, I was an Avatar. The new Avatar of this age was born shortly after I died, back in 1969."

"Has that exotic dancer in Los Angeles achieved this glorified state? Was she the avatar born in 1969?"

"Yes," said Baba.

"Have I achieved a glorified state?"

Baba looked at me blankly. I dangled my legs, hanging off the eastern edge of the table. "No, I'm afraid not," he said. "Achieving this state starts by denying one's free will. In order to achieve this state, you have to have free will. You have lost your free will. I would say you were more like the angel Moroni."

"The Mormon angel?"

"Yes," Baba continued. "Moroni was a glorified person in the form of an angel. Angels have no free will. There are seven angels. You have taken on the personality of one of those." As he said this, Baba's face morphed into that of my aunt's, waking me from my dream.

CHAPTER 26

"WHAT ARE YOU doing, layin' out here on a picnic table?" My aunt seemed angry. "I've been lookin' all over for you. You been out here with one of them Sawmill girls?"

"No Debbie."

She pulled her mouth in and filled out like a puffer fish.

"You need to be callin' me auntie. Now get your ass back up to that house before I cut it off."

On Sunday, I got up early to say goodbye to my aunt and grandma. Over breakfast, they told me the news.

"A woman's been pulled from the Kern River, some days back," said my aunt Debbie. "She'd been a stripper in LA and a prostitute up in Redding, so they suspected foul play. Seems the autopsy found traces of DNA that match that Back Alley Killer."

"The Back Alley Killer's now in Whiskey Flats," said my grandma, visibly shaken. "Samael, we're scared. We don't want you to leave."

I looked up from my Fruit Loops. "Grandma, I don't think this guy will hurt you. He kills cops and thugs."

"He could be anywhere. You need to protect us Samael."

"You're not listening. The Back Alley Killer looks for a certain type. He's a good guy, trying to cleanse the world of evil."

"Is that what you think Samael? She may have been a painted woman of the night but did she deserve to die?"

"How do you know he killed that girl? Maybe she killed herself?"

I wanted to tell them I would have never harmed Eisheth, and those others merely got their comings up.

"They found that DNA stuff, one of his hairs on her clothes, caught on the button of her shirt." My aunt was resolute.

"Anyway," I said, "he's killed a prostitute and some gang bangers. He probably won't be interested in a couple of old ladies."

"What about those police officers down in Los Angeles? The man is a cop killer."

Couldn't they see that I wasn't evil and I'd never harm an innocent? I was with Eisheth, sure, but I didn't kill her. She did that to herself. And those others, well the world is a better place without them.

"Look," I said. "I have to get back to Fairdemidland. This killer is long gone by now. You'll be ok."

I left before sun up, thinking of Eisheth as I drove north, recalling her story of the priest who paid her to have sex with him, then cast her out. I pulled into Redding, arriving at the City Church for the afternoon service. It was a vast structure, designed to lure the masses away from the Sunday game and place them before the holy tabernacle.

I looked up, across the parkinglot, to a digital sign that stood before the church, illuminating its message:

What part of "thou shall not," don't you understand?
- God

Then it flashed to a new message that read:

We need to talk.
- God

Competing with television and grade school science vs. creationism, as well as addicting images in every facet of the media, was a Sisyphean task. But it was a war the their pastor was prepared to wage. As I looked at his face on a poster that hung in the church's foyer, I knew him to be a hypocrite. He had spiked hair, a goatee and brooding male sexuality.

I was overwhelmed by the glut of humanity that piled into the place, desperate to reconcile their existence and need for worship in this crass manner.

My eyes landed on a doppelganger of Lily. Looked just like her but with fatter ass. She was pushing a pram filled to the brim with multicolored kids, whose only resemblance to their mother was her hapless eyes. I stared lovingly at her robust posterior, made ripe from rearing children for all the men who had let her into their lives. I wondered if this is what Lily would look like if we had got married and had a brood of kids?

I averted my gaze to the vulgar cathedral, whose slap up architecture convinced me of the adaptability of the Christian message. Unaware that I was blocking the isle, I looked around at the hundreds of people until the praise team took to the rostrum.

With high decibel fury, the band kicked out a driving beat, broadcasting lyrics onto a large screen. Caught up in the throws of praise, the anointed flock heralded the second coming over biting drums and pulsing guitars.

Just as I was sure the apocalypse was upon us and my frail constitution could take no more, the praise team rattled their drums and guitars. The rumble spoke of the coming onslaught, gripping me and demanding that I stay in my seat.

With a hit of the snare and a crash of the cymbal, pastor Andrews leapt on stage from some unknown point of origin. The crowd was ecstatic, lauding his celebrity with cheer and hysteria.

Then, as if the angel Gabriel descended upon him, revealing the one answer to all our questions, he unleashed his gospel into the wireless microphone.

"*Who* shall deliver us from sin?"

I was surprised. He had an English accent.

He pointed the mic to cue the crowd.

"JESUS."

"Who?"

"JESUS."

"I can't hear you."

"*Geese ussss!*"

"Now I have come here today to speak to you of the sanctity of man and woman," he said, canvassing the stage with the poise and timing of a standup comedian.

"Now I don't mean in the SEXUAL sense but the one sense that is anointed in Christ. That is, holy matrimony. For Paul tells us in Ephesians five, twenty-two, 'wives submit to your husbands as to your Lord.' "

Geese, I said to myself, this guy is a real piece of work.

"For the husband," continued Pastor Andrews, "is the head of the wife, even as Christ is the head of our church and He is the savior of its body."

I knew then, at that very moment, given the power of the Caesars, I would institute a rule of balance, altruism and kindness that would begin with a ban on institutions like the Redding City Church.

When I could just about stand no more of this misogynist sermon, he introduced a tattooed urchin, with spiky hair, as their "Extreme Youth" pastor, who hosted a special punk rock service on Monday nights for disenchanted youth.

After the worship had ended, instead of exiting the church with half of Redding California, I took to the back halls, snooping around until I found a door marked as the pastor's office. I stood alone in the hall, waiting for him to come to me. I knew it would be soon.

I heard him whistling an old Eddy Cantor show tune, jiggling his keys. He stopped when he saw me.

"Ello there. And what can I do for you?"

"Can you tell me about Jesus?" I said. I couldn't think of anything else to say.

"I really don't have time to speak to all of my parishioners but if you go down the hall to reception, they can point you in the right direction for spiritual guidance and counseling."

"I couldn't help but notice your English accent," I said. "What brings you out here?"

He put the key into his door. "The church- or as we like to call it- the *Vision*, felt that a British pastor would increase attendance. It's all about the numbers my friend, saving the most people."

"By the way," he said, opening the door to his office, "have you been saved?"

"Saved from what?" I asked.

He laughed.

"So what part of England are you from?" I didn't wait for him to turn me away but just pushed past him into his office.

"Sherwood forest."

I didn't like this guy. "Sherwood forest huh?"

"Yes, no Robin Hood there. But it's a great place for neckin'."

"Necking?"

"Yeah, you know, bag off with a bit of fluff out in the woods."

He glanced into my eyes. I must have looked repulsed. "I'm sorry, I've offended you."

"Yes you have," I said.

"Sorry ol' boy," he slapped me on the shoulder.

"You see," I said, closing the door to his office and locking it, "I knew this girl who grew up in this church. Well, they excommunicated her for something- sex scandal, I think. And it really derailed her. I look around and I don't see anyone helping people who are in moral need. There's no fostering a sense of community or work on the metaphysical enlightenment of the soul. Instead, your parish focuses on how many people you can pack into this metal framed hull of a church. Now I can't help but think, that if the priorities of this congregation were a little different, then maybe she could have been saved."

He looked nervous. "Only Jesus saves, friend."

"She accepted Jesus and hired by you to suck your cock, then you cast her from this flock. Now she's dead, threw herself into the Kern River."

He began to step back, looking around, realizing my stance had blocked his exit. We were completely alone in his office. He swallowed his spit.

"What was your friend's name?"

"Eisheth. She was a stripper and a whore. She quit all that, trying to better herself with a job at McDonalds. And what really pisses me off, is that they think I killed her."

"Oh Lord Jesus, forgive this man and deliver him from evil." He stood and backed up from his desk.

"Shh..." I said, holding my finger up to my mouth. "Don't yell or speak loudly. Try not to do anything to alarm me."

"You're the Back Alley Killer, aren't you?"

"Yes, but I would never kill an innocent person."

This seemed to calm him and he took a deep breath.

"But I didn't say that you were innocent."

In a flash, I rammed my blade into his stomach, the seat of his soul.

CHAPTER 27

I WAS BECOMING more experienced and only got the pastor's blood on my hand as he sunk behind his desk into a puddle of blood. I reached down to touch him, to feel his soul depart.

He was silent in his agony and barely spoke but managed to get out, "I... I can see a light."

"Can you see Jesus, Pastor Andrews?" I asked, putting my hands on his chest, feeling his heart rate slow.

"No."

"Didn't think you would. But don't worry pastor; God is real. Die in peace and learn from your mistakes."

They packed at least 3000 people into this church so it wasn't very personal, at best. I put my bloody hand into my pocket and made my way to the can. Everyone was so intent on being seen in their Sunday swell, that nobody seemed to notice me. I left the church, confidant that the only breach in my identity would be that damn Seattle police sketch from way back.

I was really concerned about the whole DNA thing and had the feeling that I was on the verge of getting caught. I knew the slaying of the charismatic preacher and the cops wouldn't sit well. The hounds of justice would soon be on my trail. So I hit I-5, raging north.

When I got to the outskirts of Weed, California, I parked the van and slept with the comfort, knowing that nobody but my aunt and grandma could place me in Whiskey Flats. And those two old ladies would never put the thing together.

I lay there, thinking, knowing the time had come to lay low. "I guess it's time to retire the Back Alley Killer," I said to myself.

The road to home veered off the interstate and ran north, through Bend, Oregon, all the way up to the Dalles. Then it followed the Columbia River to Fairdemidland.

Aside from the occasional oncoming traffic, I felt alone in the world, gazing at Mt. Hood and Adams out my windshield. My life would never be the same. I could never turn back the days. I was determined to stop the killings but it had become an addiction, a harmful one. I'd surely get caught. I'd left evidence.

I showed up on my mother's porch, unshaven and unannounced. She cried and held me, wondering where I'd been.

"Mom, I'm sick. I'm not well. I need a place to stay."

"You look terrible Samael. Tell me what's happened."

"I can't mom, I just can't."

"I barely recognize you, your long hair and beard. Do you want me to cut it?"

"No mom, this is how I look."

I pulled away from her fussing through my greasy hair with her fingers. She went to the couch. I sat on the floor and laid my head on her lap, crying into her dress.

"I'm in trouble. I'm having weird dreams and I feel as though some foreign force has invaded my body. I'm not well. I want so very much to be happy but I just know it's not going to happen."

"What sort of force?" asked my mother.

"An angel has possessed me. I can tell you that people believe angels are benevolent spirits. This isn't always the case. They're indifferent to good and evil. They have no free will or opinions. I've got to get it out of me."

"Sam, I think you should see a doctor."

"No, no... I'll be fine. They'll only hurt me."

"It's ok, baby," she said, stroking my hair. "I won't let anyone harm you."

"What I need is an exorcist."

The next day my mother took me to a doctor whose office sat behind *Ciao Bella's* where I used to work. Dr. Bleuler was his name. He looked just like Sigmund Freud, so I was disappointed when he failed to speak with a Viennese accent.

He asked me questions for well over an hour.

"Do you have many friends?" asked Dr. Bleuler.

"Yeah, I have two real good friends, Ted and Arbo. But I haven't been relating to them as good as I used to. I don't find joy in their company anymore."

"Do you ever see things that other people cannot see?"

"Yes. But not in the way you would think. I can look at a person and tell you when they are going to die. I have seen an avatar of God. No one else can see the divine aspect of the avatar. But I can."

"Have you spoken with this avatar?"

"Yes."

Dr. Bleuler made a note in his book. "What did the avatar say?"

"Oh, I don't know... that I'm an angel."

"Have you ever smoked cannabis?"

"Not like I used to. In fact I haven't at all in the past few months. But I smoked copious amounts before."

"Before what?"

"Before I traveled to California."

He wrote that down. I wished he hadn't done that. But I was hopeful he could help me stop the killings.

"Do you ever feel like others have control over

you?" he said in a low bedroom voice, calm like still waters.

"Angels don't have free will," I said. "I'm constantly controlled."

"So you believe you're an angel?"

"Sometimes or that an angel has entered my body, sort of like a demonic possession. But other times I know it's all bullshit."

He raised his eyebrows.

I knew I wasn't crazy but I wanted him to give me some sort of pill that would suppress the urges. I didn't want to go to jail.

Towards the end of the session, Dr. Bleuler called my mother in.

"Mrs. Giltine, your son has schizophrenia."

She started to cry.

"I refuse to accept that," I said. "I'm not crazy. There's something inside of me." I didn't know what else to do so I quit protesting and just went along with it.

"Sam," said Dr Bleuler, "you have all the symptoms. Though your positive symptoms are high, your negative symptoms are low. This means there's a good chance of living a somewhat normal life. We'll have to conduct more tests but I believe we can integrate you back into society."

I took a deep breath. "Ok," I said. "I haven't been able to function in society for a few months. I'll give it a try.

They gave me a prescription for an antipsychotic pill. I had to take four milligrams of Risperdal that made me feel like a tub of pudding. After ten days, I put my doyen knife about two feet in towards the center of my bed, between the mattress and box spring.

I had effectively retired the Back Alley Killer.

CHAPTER 28

I WAS DETERMINED to try and pick up my life where I had left it. But after you've made certain decisions or engaged in certain actions, you can never go back. But I tried. I walked down the street to the Toad bucket Café and saw the old schizophrenic Mani, just sitting out on one of the far parking curbs, smoking cigarette butts that he'd found on the ground. He didn't see me so I just went inside.

I'm not like him, I said to myself. That Dr. Bleuler is full of shit.

The girls who worked at the Bucket barely recognized me.

"Hello Janet," I said at the counter.

She looked at me in an odd way as if I were creeping up on her. Then she squinted. "Samael?"

"Yeah, how are you doing?"

"Good. Wow, you look different. Where have you been?"

I almost said California or laying in bed here in Fairdemidland. What could I tell this girl? My whole life was now a lie.

"Spokane," I said.
"What'll you have, Samael?"
"Give me a chai. Um, no, make it an Americano." I fumbled for my money.

I sat down and took a sip of my coffee. It had no taste. What was the point? The medication was sucking all the life out of me. Indifferent to it all, I looked out the widow and I saw two Mormon boys in white shirts and black ties, walking up the street toward the temple. They were on a mission.

They reminded me of the teen mother who was nursing her baby on my doorstep while trying to convert me to their Watchtower ways. Her memory began to haunt me. Instead of recalling her with disgust, I envisioned her in an angelic light. I recalled her red locks and shapely figure.

Fascinated, I abandoned my coffee and followed the two Mormon boys up the road at a discreet distance. I could see the Mormon Temple to the west, crowned by a golden angel, blowing a trumpet. I studied the two missionary boys as I walked behind. They wore white shirts, black pants and ties.

The main arterial had veered off and the traffic became scarce as we neared the temple. The building stood, surrounded by an iron fence and a lush green lawn. Its architecture was lovely and reminded me of drawings I had seen of Herod's Temple in Jerusalem.

The two boys disappeared into a red brick building that stood in the eastern lot. I walked up to the temple doors, looked up and read an inscription in the stone.

Holiness to the Lord, the house of the Lord.

I sat down on the steps, enjoying the good weather. Out came a missionary boy and sat down beside me. I looked at the poor kid, choked by this old tie. It was probably handed down to him from his Mormon dad, who lived somewhere off in Idaho or Utah.

"So," I said, already pissed off, "are you going to preach to me about Joseph Smith and Brigham Young?"

"No," said the kid.

"Oh?"

Out of nervous energy, I reached into my pocket, half expecting to find my grandfather's knife. But instead, I found a forgotten package of M&Ms.

"Care for a pocket treasure?" I said, tearing off the top of the package.

"Sure." He picked out a couple of green ones. "You're not Mormon, are you?

"No." I tossed about five M&Ms into my mouth.

"What brings you to our temple?" He had pale skin and black hair.

"I don't know," I said, sucking the hard shell to get to the chocolate and peanut center.

"Do you believe in God?"

"Oh yes," I said and I meant it.

"I don't know if I do." He was clearly tormented.

"Then why do you put on the tie and bicycle helmet to ride around for a year?"

"It's expected of me."

I looked at him, trying to read him, trying to see when he would die. Nothing. My meds had killed all my sensitivity. "Why are you telling this to me?" I said.

"You look like you'd be someone who would know all the answers."

"Really?" I leaned to the left to give him a look.

"Yeah, I saw you sitting here and you looked sort of all knowing, like an angel."

I laughed a little, tossing some more M&Ms into my mouth. "What do ya want to know, kid?"

"Is there a God?"

"Oh yes," I said, "most certainly."

"I don't know why but I believe you when you tell me this."

"That's because I've seen God and spoken with the Holy Presence."

"I can see that. You have the mark, like Moses or Zarathrushtra."

"Or Joseph Smith?"

"Yeah."

"Do me a favor, bring me out a Book of Mormon, will ya?"

"Sure." He stepped into the temple and emerged with a dark blue bound book.

"Thanks kid." I stood to take the book and turned to leave. "Your mission is a success."

I walked back to my mom's and went directly to her garage where I had a box of memorabilia. I rummaged through it and dug out that old Watchtower Magazine, held sacred from my near death bout with pneumonia. It had become the pinnacle of my purpose.

It spoke to me. I thumbed through it and read the companion article to the book of Daniel's prophesies, knowing that the whole thing must mean something, something that maybe *I* could see, but its true meaning wouldn't register to the common man or woman.

Each night I would take the Watchtower and Book of Mormon from their box and put it under my pillow to imbue me with reason while I slept.

It was noon when I awoke the next morning. I got up slow, limbs heavy with depression. The Watchtower and Book of Mormon were still under my pillow but I really didn't feel any different, other than, for the first time in years; I hadn't woke with a burning need to go to the Toad Bucket Café and get coffee.

There was a knock on my door.

"Come in."

It was my sister Amanda.

CHAPTER 29

I STARED AT Amanda blankly. She had mousey brown hair, pulled back in a ponytail with threads frizzing about on the top of her head. Looking at her, I suddenly became aware that fashions had changed.

Amanda had started her senior year in September wearing a miniskirt. With collage came this new look of flannel shirts and jeans. Work boots had replaced stiletto heels and the Risperdal had taken away my stripper god. Looking at my sister, I knew I had no future.

"Hi," she said.

"Amanda, how are you doing?" I sat up, arranging the pillows to prop myself up. "How's school?"

"Sam, are you ok?"

"Yeah, I'm all right," I said, pushing back on the headboard like a cornered rat.

"Mom called me and told me... well she told me you're sick."

"I'm not crazy." I got out of bed and put on my robe, ignoring her.

"Mom says you told the doctor that you thought you were an angel."

I didn't respond but looked away.

"Anyway," she said, "I was worried so I thought I'd come down to see you."

"Thanks." I glanced at her clothes. "You look different."

She laughed and looked down at what she was wearing.

"You look different too," she said, smiling. "You look like Kurt Cobain."

"Never heard of him."

"Don't worry, he looks cool."

"Well most people think I look like shit, except for you and this girl I met down in Redding California," I said, getting back in bed and pulling the sheet over my legs.

"So you saw grandma and Aunt Debbie?"

"Yeah."

"Mom says they're pretty worked up over that Back Alley Killer having struck down in Kernville."

I rolled my eyes.

"I guess he's working his way back up north," she said. "All my friends are rooting for him. I know; it's pretty twisted. But I'm sure after he's caught, they'll go and make a cult movie about him."

She gave me an odd look that ignited my paranoia.

"What? You haven't heard of the Back Alley Killer?"

"Yeah, I heard of him," I said.

"Well you had this look on your face."

"Sorry," I said. "It's these meds. They space me out a bit. So did you ride the bus down here?"

"No, my boyfriend drove me."

I began to worry, the rape still putting me on the defensive.

"Boyfriend? Does he treat you well?"

She laughed. "He's just like you, an angel."

She quit laughing, catching herself stumbling onto my supposed mania.

Knowing she'd already made me uncomfortable, she decided to ask more questions. "Mom also told me you were getting into Jesus."

"Just because I found God, doesn't mean I'm into Jesus."

"She says you're reading the Book of Mormon and the Jehovah Witness magazine?"

Amanda was beginning to annoy me. I picked up the Book of Mormon from the nightstand.

"Look, proof that I'm not crazy. Watch this. I'm going to take this Book of Mormon and open it to a random page and point to a passage with my eyes shut and it will be completely relevant to my claim about having a spirit of an angel inside of me."

I closed my eyes and visions of cherubim and glowing spheres appeared in my mind. I randomly opened the book, touched the page and read the sentence under my finger.

"Here, in the third Book of Nephi: 'And they (the Nephites) are as the angels of God...' The Nephites were humans who had the spirits of angels inside of them. Those Nephites were just like me."

Amanda was not impressed. "Maybe you're possessed by a demon?"

"I'm not. It's an angel. I'll try it again. Here, in Mormon chapter six: 'I made this record out of the plates of Nephi, and hid up in the hill Cumorah all the records which had been entrusted to me by the hand of the Lord, save it were these few plates which I gave unto my son Moroni.'"

"Yeah?" she raised her eyebrows. "And your point is?"

"Mormon gave a few plates to his son Moroni when he was a man."

"Isn't Moroni the angel who showed Joseph Smith the golden plates?"

"Exactly, they were one and the same."

"How can a man become an angel?"

"This is my point. Moroni was a man who had achieved angelic realization and was a glorified personage during his lifetime."

"Sam, you need a fucking exorcist, not the Book of Mormon."

"Can't be worse than these pills they got me on. Look, I'm fine. There's nothing wrong with me." I lay down on my side away from her, pulling the sheets over my head. "You and everyone else can say what they want. Did you know saints and stigmatics can share consciousness with God? Buddha and gurus can too. I share consciousness with an angel, much the same way. Smell. Can you smell the roses? They say these glorified personages smell like roses."

I could hear her softly crying. "You don't smell like roses, Sam. You smell like you need a bath. Did you take your medication today?"

"No," I admitted.

"Let me get you something to wash it down with."

She returned, handing me my pill and a glass of water. That's how it was for the next five years.

CHAPTER 30

5 years later

BECAUSE OF THE meds, I dropped out for about five years. I no longer had anything in common with my old friends. My whole purpose had been wrapped up in the "angelic nature" thing, flying with the eagles. And like Moses, I yearned to look into the sun and see your face. How it would burn.

I wandered the streets, depressed and nervous.

Without self-confidence and motivation, I began to wither. The medication kept me low. Some days my limbs felt so heavy, I stayed in bed until nightfall. I got a job installing blinds so I could work alone, not talk to anybody.

What's been keeping me on this earth, I just don't know? For the past five years, at times, I have felt like giving up.

One day I went to the Toad Bucket Café. None of the same girls worked there. They'd gotten married or graduated from university. It just wasn't the same. I tried to go out and meet somebody. It seemed there wasn't a woman alive who could interest me, not that they'd have anything to do with me anyway.

After you, there is none.
Then one day, I decided to quit taking my meds. I had been laid off from my job and felt it time for some changes. Within days, the urge to reconnect with my old life returned and I reached under my mattress and pulled out granddad's switchblade.

I called up Ted Salinger to see if he was still alive. Seems the dope had preserved his flesh like a vampire, extending his life and making his skin look like a manikin's.

"Some junkies live forever," he told me.

"Want to meet for coffee?"

"Nah, Janet graduated from collage and they got some woman managing the place that hires nothing but dudes and old broads. How about a beer at *Raymond's*?"

"I guess. My doctor doesn't want me to drink but I suppose it wouldn't hurt to meet you."

Raymond's was this obnoxious bar where they played punk rock and the place still smelled of smoke seven years after the indoor cigarette ban. The music there was loud, piercing my eardrums.

"Hey," I yelled over the crap band, "Where's Arbo these days?"

"Oh, he's running this pizza place, *New York Thin Slice*. Got himself a real young doll he's shacked up with and they're living up town. We call her, Little Red."

"Yeah, I think I met her before I left."

He waved me outside.

"Come on, I need a cigarette."

He pulled out a Camel and lit it with a chrome Zippo.

"Yep," he said, sucking in the flame, "he's still Arbo, grumpy as fuck. What are you up to Sam?"

"Nothin' Ted. I feel about hopeless. I've changed a good deal since I've left Fairdemidland. I'm just not the same guy I used to be."

Ted looked at me, taking a drag. "I'll say you're not the same guy. You look like you play for Motorhead or Hawkwind. Look Samael, come on in and I'll buy you a cola or juice."

I followed Ted into the seedy bar, feeling like I was about to suffocate and walked past a girl who recognized me and put her arms around my neck.

"Sam Giltine!"

I had no idea who she was. She had this short styled hair, similar to the look my grandma sported back in the day and she was about three times my size.

"Geese Sam, I haven't seen you since high school. How's Amanda?"

"She's cool, going to college up in Pullman. Someone in our family has to get an education." I still had no idea who she was.

"I almost didn't recognize you with all that long hair. You look like you've been hanging out with Ted a little too much."

"Funny, I haven't seen Ted in over five years."

"Where've you been?" She eyed me head to toe.

"Around." I said.

It finally dawned on me who she was. Her name was Candice and I used to date her in school. She dumped me because she suspected I was in love with Lily Jahl. She was right.

"Come, have a drink with me sweetie," she said, giving me that flirty eye.

"Probably shouldn't. I'm driving and I can't afford even a minor hassle from the cops."

I didn't want to tell her about my condition. I should've because the wine coolers coursing through her veins caused her to feel slighted.

"Fuck you, Sam."

"But…"

She walked off.

I turned to Ted, who was laughing. "First night out and you're doin' great."

"Yeah, real great. Ted, I best be goin'. Hanging around all this booze makes me want to drink."

"Alright man. Drop in on Arbo."
"Ok, I will."
I walked out of the bar and there was Candice smoking.
"Screw you Samael," she said, blowing out smoke as I walked by. "You're probably still in love with Lily Jahl. You deserve her. If only you could see her now. You wouldn't think she's so hot."
Her words gripped my heart and twisted. She looked at me and laughed. Must have been the look on my face.
"You don't know, do you Sam?"
"Know what?" I was horrified and opened my eyes wide, fearing what she would say. But I had to listen. I was held too tight by the past just to turn and walk away.
Candice walked up to me, swanky and confident, determined to bury me low.
"I'll tell you where you can find Lily so you can go and know for certain that you gave the best years of your life to a worthless piece of trash. She lives in a trailer court on the outskirts of Fairdemidland."
"The one out on 9th Line?" I swallowed hard, my heart agitating and in pain.
"You can't miss it," Candice said. "Go and see her Sam."
"Is she married?"
She just laughed. "Eat crow and go fuck yourself." She walked back into the bar, throwing her cigarette down on the asphalt.
I didn't want to see Lily but I felt the urge to go. My feelings were tearing me apart, wanting to love her and hurt her all at the same time. It was late and she was probably at home. I could go to her.
There I stood, my love for that hapless slut Lily, pulling me down. I reached into my pocket and there was my grandpa's switchblade, vibrating, demanding me to give it attention like a small child.

CHAPTER 31

I WALKED ACROSS the street to an all-night gas station to buy a *Snickers* bar and some nachos.

"Say, do you have a *White Pages*?"

The guy looked at me like I was scum. He frowned, reaching under the counter, chewing gum with his mouth open and slapped the worn and frayed phone book in front of me.

"Here, but you can't use the phone. It's against store policy."

I didn't reply, just fed through the pages to J. There it was, L. Jahl, #32 Path Rd.

"I shouldn't do this," I said to myself. "Just leave it be, Samael. Let it go."

Cramming nachos into my mouth, I went back to my van, hoping to get Lily off my mind and ease the calling. I began to cry. Maybe I could put off going to her by driving up to that pie house to see Arbo?

"No," I cried, piloting my van. "Go and see Arbo. Leave it be. Forget that bitch. She's not worth it."

I walked in to the pizza place and there he was, covered in flour, wearing a white apron, stained with sauce.

"Samael!" Arbo came around the counter and hugged me. "I thought I told you never to come back to this shit hole?"

"You know how it is, you're never really done with Fairdemidland."

"Yeah." He laughed. "But it sure is good to see you."

"How is it working here?" I said.

"Sucks. You can't drink on the job but snorting coke doesn't seem to be a problem. It's not the type of environment that I thrive in."

He had that cocaine look in his eye as he ran the back of his hand along his runny nose.

"How much does it pay?"

He laughed. "Don't ask. As long as you don't know, you don't mind. Boss gives draws for drinking money and you get paid every Friday so you can never save enough cash to quit. It's a bigger trap then Fairdemidland."

He began hitting the flour off his apron.

"I hear your still with that girl."

"Little Red? God I love her."

I could tell that he had found a greater affection for this girl than he had for whiskey and Hank Williams.

"So where you been, Samael? I heard rumors for the past few years that you were in town."

Again, I didn't know what to say.

"I've been to Hell," I said. "No Arbo, that's not right. I've been to heaven and discovered God for myself."

He blinked and looked at me for several seconds, then let out a laugh. "You still are a hoot."

I hung around a bit, watching these guys toss their pizza dough and deal with their customers until I could stand no more and got up to leave. "Well Arbo, I've got to go. I'll be in touch."

"Quit being a stranger, ok."

I got back in my van, yearning to go and see Lilith Jahl.

"Oh Lily, what that horrid chick Candice said about

you. I've got to see you. I'm just afraid of what I might do."

I made my way out to 9th Line. It was dark and I could see the Fairdemidland water tower, illuminated in the distance. Next to it, the trailer park, surrounded by desert. Airstreams, campers and busses, a few doublewides, it wouldn't be too hard to find her.

Then I saw it, #32. It was late but the lights were on so I drove by, too afraid to stop, hyperventilating with anxiety. I looped around and drove by again. The gravel road crumbling under my wheels was amplified by the van's hull. The noise alerted the entire community to my approach so I parked and got out on foot, putting my hand in the pocket of my blue jeans. There she was, grandpa's knife, the sole tool of my trade. The neighborhood was dark, save for a lone streetlamp illuminating the gravel intersection. I stared at it for a moment, observing the crossroads like a hypnotic vision from a past life.

I walked up to her mailbox and opened it. It was stuffed with three day's worth of mail. I pulled out an envelope. A utility bill addressed to Lilith Jahl. My sweaty hand left a damp print on it, evidence. I put the bill into my coat pocket and turned my attention back to the modular home and gently climbed the stairs with padded steps to peep into her window.

The curtain was open and I could see a couple of kids planted about two feet in front of the television screen. On the other side of the window was the back of Lily's head. She was stuffing her face with "No Brand" potato chips. A third child, a toddler, was half heartedly playing in the corner and stopped every so often to watch the TV. Seems his will was held captive by the images of sex and violence coming off the screen.

I stood there for a while, feeling a slight welling of a tears but not a full cry. I loved this woman and I hated her at the same time. I should have been the father of these kids, knowing full well, I would be chaining myself to a vital hell. Could it be worse than the hell I walked through daily?

Some folks are just born condemned.

She let her brother rape my sister. She ignored me, was rude to me in passing and yet, I wanted her, wanted her more than anything I ever came upon in all my days.

I stepped back and the rotten deck creaked. The sound of my feet on her porch alerted her dog. The beast leapt up with paws planted on the back of the couch, barking at me through the window.

Lily turned and saw me standing there on her front porch. Should I run?

Knowing I had no freewill, the angel inside me moved up to the door and slowly knocked. Lily opened. She had greasy hair and wore soiled sweat pants. She had not aged well, letting her looks slide.

The dog stood next to her, barking. I could relate to this beast. It was loyal and vigilant. He would love Lily, regardless, keeping her safe.

"Shut up," Lily yelled, kicking the dog in the ribs.

He whined and growled quietly behind her. I still had my hand on the knife, tempted to plunge it into her unfeeling heart.

"What do you want?" she said. "I don't take newcomers without a referral and I don't do a job without you calling first."

"Sorry," I said, not knowing what she was talking about.

"Lucky for you, I need the money. Come on in." She gruffly motioned me through the door.

I walked into her home. It smelled like dog and stale cigarettes. I could see into the kitchen. The dishes were piled in the sink and old pizza boxes and Mickey D's bags lined the counter, along with beer cans and soiled diapers.

The kids ignored me and the young one in the corner smelled like he needed to be changed.

"Pause that movie, momma's got to work."

"Can we play *Nintendo*?" said the oldest; whom I figured might be on the high end of four years.

"I don't care."

She turned to me without looking my way and said, "Let's go."

I followed her into her bedroom and she shut the door.

"I get paid up front." She had her hand out, gaze turned to the wall. I was stunned. She was whoreing herself out in front of her kids.

I stroked the blade in my pocket. "How much?" is all I could say.

"Thirty bucks."

"Lilith, it's me, Sam."

She looked at me for the first time since she'd opened her front door.

"Who?"

"Samael Giltine, Amanda's brother."

She turned and walked toward the bed, trying to process what I had said.

"Oh yeah. But that don't mean you get a discount. It's still thirty bucks."

I had a fifty in my wallet. Lily took the money and stuffed it into the pocket of her sweat pants, neglecting to give me change. She pulled her pants down to her ankles, pushing each leg off with the opposite foot, revealing that she had gotten fat and her skin was no longer creamy. Like twenty-two going on seventy, she no longer had the shape.

It didn't matter, my heart pined and I yearned to hold her in my arms. She would always be perfect in my eyes.

Lilith lay down on her unmade bed and looked at me standing there like a rabbit in her headlights.

"Hurry up and get your pants off. I want to get back to my show."

I stared at her lying there, legs fatter then they'd ever been, poking out from an oversized t-shirt.

"Don't you want to talk first," I said, voice shaking.

"Just because I used to hang out with your sister

doesn't mean we've got anything to say. If you want to fuck, let's fuck. If you want to talk, I'm givin' you fifteen minutes, then I'm back to my movie."

I took off my clothes and climbed on top of her. I wasn't even hard. I was scared. Her bed sheets smelled of body odor and I could feel crumbs under my palms as I held myself up. I tried to kiss her but she turned away. So I followed her, trying again but she flung her face in the opposite direction.

"I don't kiss nobody. Let's just do this."

I reached up into her shirt. She pulled out my hand.

"I've got stretch marks."

"Lily, I don't mind. You've always been beautiful to me."

"Whatever," she said. "*I* care about the stretch marks and I ain't beautiful. If you're going to fuck me, then fuck me. If not, climb off."

I tried but I was in limbo.

"You shrivel dick," she said. "You're just bumpin' the pussy. I'm going back to my show and don't expect a refund."

"Lily, I don't want a refund."

My love for her began to swell in my breast. I hugged her tight. "Lilith, will you marry me?"

"Husband and wife role playing will cost extra," she said.

"Lily, I'm serious. I'll be a father to your kids."

"Get the fuck off me, Samael. I'm gonna watch my movie. You can let yourself out."

I got out of her bed and began to shake, weak in my step, stumbling as I reached for my trousers, feeling a heartsick pain enter each cell of my flesh. Lily grabbed her pants with a yank and stepped out into the living room to get dressed in front of her kids.

My lip quivered and chin crinkled as I began to cry. "Oh Lord, why can't I be happy and live in peace?"

I stood there, naked from the waist down, weeping

buckets as Lily changed the TV screen from Nintendo to her movie, the kids shouting protests.

"Shut up. Momma's gonna watch her show."

I put on my pants and stepped out into the living room.

"Momma, why's that man crying?"

"What man?" said Lily. "There's no man. This guy is just a boy punk who doesn't exist."

I ran out and slammed their door before my flailing emotions caused me to slit her throat, kicking the side of my van so hard; I must've broken my toe. I didn't care.

"God, why do you treat me so?" I cried, flooring it out of her trailer park, spraying gravel all over her yard of weeds,

"Because you are my servant, my Angel of Death," said a voice in my head. "And I want you to get back to work."

CHAPTER 32

THE NEXT MORNING was pretty depressing. My emotions were still sore from Lily. Needing to get my mind off it, I sponged five bucks off my mom and walked down the road to the Toad Bucket Café.

The staff was all gathered around a newspaper that sat in front of the espresso bar, talking and ignoring their customers.

"He killed a girl again last night," said the woman, who now managed the place. "It's just terrible."

"They were all whores," said the barista, wiping his hands on his black apron.

"Mark, don't be crude. Look, we've got a customer."

I sighed, knowing that the service and the quality had left with Janet.

"Sorry, we didn't see you," said the manager.

"That's ok," I said, hands in my pockets. "What were you talking about, if you don't mind me asking?"

"The Moth," said Mark.

"A new serial killer has broken out." The manager handed me the paper. "He's killed three women in three months. He's on an unstoppable rampage."

"Whores and strippers," added Mark.

"The first one was a sorority girl." She glared at him.

"A skank of a different kind," he said.

My hands shook, reading the headlines.

Thee dead in three months.
Killer vows to strike again during next full moon.

His second victim was a stripper from Seattle. I stared at her photo with compassion.

"Such a waste," I said. "I wish I had known her."

My comment seemed to unsettle the people working there. I took the paper and stepped out of the order line.

The killer had sent a letter to the Seattle Times with unpublished details from the crime scene. With churning belly, I read the freak's statement:

I burn like a star exploding
I glow like the sun
To mow people over with poison rays
and return to where I was born, made by foolish men.

But by night, I am the Moth.

I stared at the print with my mouth agape. I somehow knew what he was talking about. It was as if I had a special insight, as if our lives were lived in tandem or parallel. We were spiritually connected.

I was the Eagle; he was the Moth. I flew into the sun and he by the moon. It was as if I knew him and could feel his motions. He had killed a girl last night behind a cheap motel. She was a prostitute. The words jumped out at me, making my skin pimple.

Authorities are split on their opinions. The Seattle police believe the killings to be the work of the dormant Back Alley Killer or that of a copycat. But Special Agent Broderick of the FBI's Behavioral Science Unit, claims the new killer is more organized and is trying to make it look as though he were being random.

"The Moth is an organized Lust Killer," said Broderick. "He takes pride in his slayings and contacts the media. The Back Alley Killer is a Vision Killer who is most likely asexual. His killings have been random, with the exception of the LAPD officer. He wants to remain anonymous and is most likely schizophrenic."

I turned the page, only to be faced with a picture of the new victim. Horror shot through me.

"I know this girl," I said loudly, pointing to the paper.

Conversations throughout the café stopped. The employees looked up. Everyone stared at me.

"Oh God," I cried. "I know her. She's been killed?"

"You knew Ginny Simmons?" asked the barista, Mark.

"Who?" I squinted at him.

I looked down to the photo. The caption said it was Ginny Simmons but there was no mistaking the black hair and almond eyes.

"This girl isn't Ginny Simmons. The newspaper is wrong. Her name is Kali. I should know, I used to date her."

Conversations resumed.

"Her name's Kali," I shouted.

"Ok Sam," said Mark. "You know the drill. If you're going to start ranting nonsense in the café, then you'll have to leave."

"I'm ok," I said, tapping the side of my temple with my middle finger to clear my thoughts and calm myself. "I'll behave. Let me stay."

"Maybe next time Sam. It's time to go."

"But he killed Kali," I said. "It's her, I'm telling you."

I left the Bucket, heading home. I can't really explain it any other way then by saying that I felt a connection to this killer. It was like I could smell this creep from a distance. Basically, the Moth was dangerous and I could stop him. It would be my redemption and I knew in my heart that I would catch him before the police, for they lacked my insight.

This was my new purpose. I would never again take antipsychotic medication.

CHAPTER 33

THE FIRST VICTIM'S body was found floating face down in a pool in Cle Ellum, where the Yakima River diverts into many large ponds and tributaries. She was a coed at Central Washington University.

He was looking for his type. Probably couldn't get it up with the average girl so he tried a sorority slut. I thought about my sister, going to school up in Pullman. This jerk had to be stopped.

The second Moth killing had taken place in Seattle, on the shores of Lake Washington, down the street from a strip club where the victim had been working. He had tied the girl to a boat dock and left her there, floating dead and naked for everyone to see.

I closed my eyes, trying to think of why he would do such a thing instead of hiding the body.

"You're cocky, aren't you?" I said to the newspaper. "You like to show off." I was beginning to build my own profile. I thought about the pole dancing Avatar of God. The Moth made me angry.

The third killing was a streetwalker from *Yakima*, Ginny Simmons, but I knew her as Kali. The Moth tied

Kali's body to an Indian fishing scaffold outside the town of Desert Aire, eleven miles from the ghost town where she claimed to live. I had to avenge Kali. Eisheth was a streetwalker at one point. I hated this killer.

"I see you're moving from strippers to whores, trying to find your type," I said, taking out a map and marking off the spots where he had struck.

He was working his way east, and each time he abducted the women in daylight. He would wait for nightfall and then take them next to a body of water where he would rape and murder them. He did his thing by night.

I closed my eyes and tried to imagine him but his face was black.

He has to see to hunt but kills his prey at night, I thought. He needs the water, not just any water but water like the Delta here in Fairdemidland. I'm going to catch him. I can feel it.

I had learned all I could from the press clippings and knew I needed to visit the crime scenes. The next morning, I borrowed one hundred dollars from my mother and drove my van out of town for the first time in five years. I arrived at the third crime scene, Desert Aire, in just a quarter over an hour.

Parking at the local filling station, I walked right up to the yellow tape, portioning off the murder site by the shore. The FBI was busy scouring the area.

This is where Kali had died. I slumped over, feeling a pain in my chest. "I'm going to hunt and kill this son of a bitch."

The Moth would be powerless to stop me. I could smell him as I watched the feds pick the place apart in vain.

"Can I help you?" came a voice from behind.

I turned around with a start. It was a fed, in his FBI jacket, holding a Styrofoam cup of coffee.

"You scared me," I said, putting my hand on my chest. "Is this where the Moth killed that girl?"

"Sir this is a crime scene, not a tourist attraction. We can't have you loitering around sight seeing."

"Right," I said, turning to leave. "Sorry."

He shook his head in disgust. I got in my van and crossed the Columbia at I-90, making my way to Cle Ellum.

This crime scene was harder to find so I drove around until I came right up to an FBI roadblock. An agent approached and I rolled down my window.

"Sorry, this area's closed due to an investigation."

"No prob," I said, turning around.

Two hours later I was in Seattle, driving up the arterial to the first crime scene. I drove until I saw a large neon sign shaped like a pair of legs in fishnet stockings. It was the strip joint where the Moth's second victim had worked. I followed the road to this exclusive neighborhood by the lake where I could see the FBI investigators foraging about. I got out and watched them.

All three crime scenes had a familiar quality to them. They all had calm water and reminded me of the Yakima River Delta back in Fairdemidland, a place indigenous to a moth.

I turned to make my way back up to the strip club that the victim had danced in. As I unlocked my van, an FBI agent approached me.

"Sir, this is a crime scene. I'm going to have to ask you to leave."

"Sorry, I just wanted to go for a walk along the beach but couldn't find a path. As you can see, I'm about to leave."

I drove up to the strip club. As I opened the brass handled door, the sounds of the street traffic were overwhelmed by some 80s hard rock song blasting from the club's PA through the open door. A greasy guy in a white shirt and vest with a slick backed ponytail stopped me at the door.

"Five dollar cover."

"Here," I said, handing him the bill.

It was brutally dark and there were a lot of empty round tables with an old guy or two, sitting about, nursing their drinks, trying to prolong buying another. A blonde haired girl with a healthy body was spinning around a brass pole, looking bored.

My palms began to sweat. Feeling timid and uncomfortable, I tried to sit in an inconspicuous chair in the shadows. A girl in a vest, fishnets and panties with a money belt came up holding a tray.

"What can I get you?"

"A whiskey and Coke."

"Sorry fella, there's no alcohol served in strip clubs in Washington State."

"Then I'll just have a Coke."

Girls were seated along the back wall in the dark. You could barely make them out. The girl dancing rotated upside down around the pole like a toy.

I could feel a pair of eyes riveted to the back of my head. I turned to look behind. It was you, the pole dancing, rollerblading Avatar of God. You stood, like you were rising up from the primordial fount and walked toward me, sliding your hand over my shoulder. You were wearing a sapphire thong with matching cups on your brassiere and earthen tone boots.

"Would you care for a lap dance?" you said.

"Yes." I was choking on your intention.

"Come with me to the VIP Lounge."

You led me into a back area where silhouettes of young girls hovered over old men's bellies, grinding to the beat of the dollar. You placed me on a portioned off couch and straddled me, sitting on my thighs and grinding into my loins.

"Am I sick?" I asked.

"Why would you be sick?" You bent down to whisper in my ear with your arms around my neck.

"Because I think you're a hallucination."

"Feel me, I'm real." You grabbed my hands and placed them on your bounty - the hips that felt plump and the thighs that felt like silk, yet firm as stone.

"But you were in Los Angeles and now you're here?"

You didn't answer but seemed emotionless and detached, floating above me, not once looking me in the eye. I just gazed up into your majesty and beauty as you pushed your tits into my face.

"I want to catch a bad man who's killing women," I said into your cleavage.

"The Moth?"

"Yes."

"You won't find him here. He won't hit the same place twice. I saw him the night he killed Marsha. He sat right where you're sitting. Marsha straddled him just like I'm straddling you." You took my hands and placed them over your sapphire cups. "He felt her tits, just like you're feeling mine." You pushed into my groin but I felt no carnal stimulation. It was just a soul communing with its maker, nothing sexual about it.

"Marsha's problem," you said, "was that she was prone to giving up the diamond. In this business, you should never give up the diamond. And now she's dead."

"Are you God?" I asked.

You squinted at the question, lifted yourself up and pushed your ass into my stomach and chest. After turning back around to straddle me, you said, "We are all an expression of God and yet we are all independent and unique. I am a human, and like you, I have achieved a glorified state. When I close my eyes, I can see everything at once. I am the master of reality but in control of none."

I lifted my head as you ran your hand along my jaw, swaying to the music. "I can tell you where you'll find the man you seek."

"Where?" I sat up, tense.

"He is traveling. His next stop will be on the banks of the Spokane River where it empties into the Columbia, at Fort Spokane. The Moth hunts to purge unwanted desires, defiling his prey. I want you to hunt him with sanctimonious reverence. Be merciless."

The song ended and you looked down upon me and said, "Aren't you forgetting something?"

"What?"

"That'll be twenty dollars."

"Oh... sure." I pulled out my wallet, my hands trembling as I fumbled through the bills. You took the money and stood up, emotionless, walking into the shadows where you evaporated from my sight. All happiness dropped from my body like water spiralling down a drain. I began to cry. The bouncer was staring at me and approached, looking tuff.

"If you are going to behave oddly, you're going to have to leave."

"Sorry," I said, breaking away. "I'm going."

I left, knowing that my time had come. The Moth would be my encore, my final act of brilliance, my masterpiece. Putting Seattle behind me, I made my way east on I-90 towards Spokane.

After Ritzville, I turned off onto a country road that took me through a couple of slow moving towns with names like Harrington and Davenport. Through prairie on up to timberland mountains, then down into the river valley- I drove until I came upon the site of old Fort Spokane.

The fort was now a tourist attraction. There was a big car park for the recreation area where there was a boat launch. It was off-season and the place was deserted.

I pulled over and looked about. "Not here," I said. Across the river I saw a casino. "That's where he'll strike."

Getting out of my van, I walked toward the casino's entrance. I was greeted by the hum of computer slot machines, sucking the life from human zombies, held within a cacophony of fractal clicks.

An old woman, sitting next to her walker and a tank of oxygen that kept her alive, was connected to the great slot idol by a spiral orange plastic cord. I looked on in horror as the cord ran from her wrist to a memory card inserted into the digital beast. It was her lifeline, connecting her to her craven lord, sustaining her more than her oxygen tank ever could.

In heated fervor, she bet, laying more money down than I could make in a week. I wanted to reach out and pull her gambling plug but it would probably kill her and I needed to save that sort of thing for the Moth.

We kept walking. It was like Babylon of old, Mecca before Mohammad and the Spokane Indians were the Qureshi, keepers of the key, counting their money while the towns of Davenport and Harrington lay asleep down river.

There were a few women standing about. Not street whores but women who could be bought. I knew this, as did the Moth. I looked at each of them, wondering which one he would choose. What would be his taste: the blonde; the red head; the native girl?

These women are of a higher caliber, I thought. The Moth will try and get hard for one of them. Was he here? I looked at each face, wondering if I could recognize murder in his eyes.

"It's now fully dark," I said to myself. "It won't be here. Make your way down to the river. Stand guard in vigilance, hiding in the shadows. Wait for him to come. It will be soon."

I left the casino and made my way down to the river. An hour passed. The only sound was the crickets. I was about to give up and return to the casino, when I heard the sounds of footfall on weeds and twig. I became alive and reached for my knife.

My predator instincts were ready to pounce. I could make out a silhouette. The Moth?

I heard the arming of a gun.

"Freeze, FBI. Keep your hands where I can see them."

Out of the night came five men in black jackets and pistols. I dropped my knife.

"No," I said, stepping back with my hands up. "You're making a mistake."

As they cuffed me and read my rights, I looked off into the darkness and I could swear that I saw two eyes glowing like the moon. It was the Moth.

"Stop," I yelled, digging in my heels. "He's out there, right behind us. The man you want is there."

The FBI dragged me along, up the hill.

I was in custody and the Moth was watching us, at large by the river. I looked back and it began to snow.

CHAPTER 34

THE IRONY OF life, I have killed eight men: one transient, four muggers, two brutal cops and a hypocritical judgmental priest. And here I sat in the Spokane Indian Reservation's Sheriff's office, accused of raping and killing innocent women.

These stupid cops had the notorious Back Alley Killer in their custody, slayer of eight, accused of ten, and they thought I was the Moth, killer of three.

My problem was that these overly observant bastards had seen me at all three of the crime scenes. The FBI's Behavioral Science Unit felt as I did, that the Moth would strike at some Eastern Washington river delta.

I noticed a difference between these FBI cops and the regular cop on the beat. These cops weren't afraid. They were big time and secure with their power. They were intelligent, and despite foiling my plans, I liked them very much.

They had lots of questions:
"Did you kill Celia Grant?"
"No."
"Marsha North?"

"No."

"Did you kill Ginny Simmons?"

"No, I'm not the Moth."

"Why were you at all three crime scenes?"

"I told you, morbid curiosity. I'm an amateur sleuth. I wanted to catch him."

A man in a navy blue suit walked in, causing commotion with the energy he brought into the room. He seemed to upset my interrogators. He had short brown hair and certain amount of polish.

"I got here as soon as I could," he said. "Can I have a moment alone with Mr. Giltine, please?"

The other agents got up to leave. He sat directly across from me and when I looked into his eyes I could see the mark of the brotherhood of predators. We were kin and shared the same function, had the same motivations and needs. The difference: he was higher up the food chain and I was his prey.

"Mr. Giltine. May I call you Sam?"

"Yes."

"Sam, my name's Special Agent Broderick."

I recognized his name. He was the FBI's top profiler on serial killers. He'd profiled me.

"How long have you been here, Sam?"

"Not sure, at least thirteen hours."

"14.5, to be exact. Do you understand what it is you are being accused of?"

"You believe me to be the Moth."

"No," he chuckled to himself. "They believe you to be the Moth." He pointed out the door with his thumb. "I think your something different."

"What do you think I am?" I sat back in my chair.

"A vigilante, someone trying to track the Moth; trying to beat me to the punch. Lucky for you, the Moth just struck up river, west of Hunters, while we held you here. I guess this absolves you of suspicion." He looked me in the eye and smiled. "Suspicion of the Moth murders; that is. We're waiting for your DNA sample to come back."

He was the cat and I the mouse. He was toying with me.

"The Moth is impotent, trying to cure himself. I don't believe that you'd ever rape a woman. I think you're a-sexual."

I looked at him intently, not even bothered about what he said. He was right about me and in my heart, I too believed the Moth to be impotent. This Broderick and I shared similar faculties.

"As it stands, we've got nothing on you and I have to release you. Can I give you a ride to your car?"

"Sure," I said.

I could tell he knew who I was. You could see it in his pleasantries as he drove to Fort Spokane.

"So you were born in Fairdemidland?" he said, eyes on the road.

"Yes."

I didn't want to talk to him. He drove so slow that the scenery outside seemed to creep by, agonizing me.

"I was born in Yakima so it's nice being back in the Pacific Northwest. I spend most of my time in Washington D.C. What do you do for a living, Sam?"

"I used install blinds and drapes. Now I'm unemployed."

"That's right. I remember. You worked in a restaurant before window coverings or was it phone work, conducting movie surveys or something like that?"

I was astonished.

"We ran your Social Security number. The FBI has a file on just about everyone."

He knew the answers to all his questions. He was putting me through some sort of psychological assessment.

"Are you a religious man, Sam?"

I remembered his profile of me stated that he believed the Back Alley Killer to be religious. I thought about the question for a while, feeling him observe me, making mental notes.

"I am," I said, "but I *don't* go to church."

"The Moth has offended your religious sensibilities, hasn't he?"

"What do you mean?"

"Well, you hunt this man, as do I. It's a spiritual thing for you, isn't it?"

I didn't answer him.

"I would venture to say that you practice some sort of animism."

"I don't know what that is," I said.

"No? Well sometimes I get a little ahead of myself. No matter. It is the belief that God animates the material world, giving everything; even inanimate objects and animals a soul. Basically everything is an expression of God."

He drove up next to my van and brought his car to a patient stop. I got out and he rolled down his window.

"Samael Maximon Giltine, it was a pleasure meeting you. Just stay out of my hunting grounds. I feel I know you Mr. Giltine. I'm sure we'll be meeting each other again. I know a killer when I see one, because I'm a killer myself. I've shot and killed six men in the line of duty and my greatest successes as a profiler have come in the states that have the death penalty- logging my personal death toll at twenty one. You see; it's my passion. I love to kill another human being. But I butcher men within the confines of Federal and State legislation. I'll get you Samael. Why? Because they have the death penalty in Washington State. Now go and run. Give me the sport that a hunter of my stature deserves."

I stood looking at him, the wind blowing my long hair.

"Why are you letting me go?"

He laughed. "I could say that it's because I'm busy with the Moth. He rapes and kills women. Whatever you are, you prey on lesser predators, possibly even leaving the streets a safer place. He's a larger priority and you'd get in the way. I could even say that your capture in conjunction with the Moth would possibly dilute my media spotlight but all that's bullshit. It's just that I didn't want to catch you this way. It would take all the fun out of it. Now run Samael, let me chase you properly."

He rolled up his window and contrary to the way he came, he tore out of the empty parking lot and off into the Spokane Indian Reservation, spraying snow and leaving me standing there, shaking.

It was as though he'd raped me.

Snow was falling and I was worried about making it back to Fairdemidland. I got into my van, ignited the engine and began to cry.

I was defeated.

Or was I? Broderick had issued the challenge but sucked my confidence and drive.

It was a tormenting drive home. I got in very late and it stormed all night.

The next morning I woke depressed, drained of all reason for life. I had trouble getting out of bed and left the house unclean, without purpose. I didn't want to go out but I knew that I couldn't stay another minute. They were closing in on me. When the DNA would come in, the entire FBI would be at my mom's door. I was done and I hadn't caught the Moth. I was being denied my masterpiece.

It would be good to walk it off so I drove to the park. Kids were sledding on the hill, yelling and shouting with glee. Despite the cold snow at my feet, the scene warmed my jaded heart.

For the first time in my life, I wished I had kids. The only girl I could imagine having kids with is you, if that's even possible, or Lily, had she ever wanted me. Then I recalled that her brother raped my sister. How I have loved in vain and had it turned back on me, perverted to black. Yet, might I still be capable of love, had not all been lost?

My time was up. I was done.

If only I hadn't ran into Kali or seen the eagle or seen you. Maybe then, I could be happy, but alas, I am but a servant of the Lord.

I stood at the bottom of the hill, off to the side, as parents waited and conversed, their children going up and sledding down continuously. For a brief moment I was happy. Then darkness crept into my heart.

"I could be anyone," I said under my breath. "A child molester; the Moth. Hell, I'm the Back Alley Killer."

These parents took no inventory and assumed I was one of them, waiting on his kids. I became annoyed by their lack of vigilance.

"Dangerous men about," I said to myself.

I also felt guilty deriving pleasure from the scene; regardless of how innocent my intentions were. I was convinced that there was no more innocence left in the world.

My gloomy considerations were interrupted by a girl of about six years, ripping down the hill on a sleigh fully out of control. In a moment of brash decision, she abandoned the toboggan, letting it slide down the hill without her.

Her mother ran for the renegade sled.

"Wow, that was fun." The girl grabbed the toboggan and went for another go.

"Careful sweetie," said her mother.

"I know," said the child with an authoritative tone, resembling an adult. "It requires balance."

I smiled, finding this child to be glorious. Then I took notice of her mother.

The woman was beautiful. I don't think a mortal woman has ever moved me more than this. For the first moment in my life, I was free of Lily Jahl and her siren's spell. This woman was definitely made in your image. She had long corkscrew hair and an angelic face. I was smitten.

Her posture and stride were immaculate. How I yearned to touch her lips, caress her cheek. I could cry on her shoulder and she could exorcise all my demons with her exquisite grace. A woman like her could redeem me.

I caught myself staring at her amorously, without restraint as she looked after her beautiful child. Embarrassed, I lowered my gaze, feeling like a stalker or a pervert.

Had I become so jaded with bloody hands that I couldn't even enjoy human beauty in innocence without digging up or inventing some ulterior motive? I turned away from them. She's too good for you, I thought, and you're doomed anyway.

I turned back. I shouldn't have felt guilty. I had no designs on this woman. I was merely admiring her qualities and the love of a mother and child.

I looked at her again. She began to look familiar. Where had I seen this angel of mercy before?

It's not possible. If I had seen her before, I would have remembered her and burnt her image into my heart. I could love a woman like this and cherish her. Yet it was undeniable, I knew her.

Then it hit me.

I felt a chill run from my scalp to my boot. I did know her. She, this perfect creature and her lovely child, were no other than that dirty-legged teenage dropout Jehovah Witness girl. And this child, sledding down the hill was the baby that sucked on that tit out in front of my house, that day, so many years ago.

They were the ones who had given me the Watchtower Magazine.

CHAPTER 35

I TURNED TO run as my whole world came crashing down upon my very being. I slipped and fell, face first, into the snow.

Oh God, how can this be? Am I wrong, wrong about so many things?

The snow stung my face and the fall hurt my knee.

"Oh Lord," I said aloud, "Forgive me. Given the power of Nero, I would have thrown all the Jehovah Witnesses to the lions. Am I a murderer or an executioner?"

"Both," said a voice in my head.

Running into her and this child and viewing how they had matured and grown, could not have been coincidence.

I lifted myself up off the snow. I knew this woman held the answers to all my questions. She was the modern Madonna of my visions and the feeling hung over me like a swarm of gnats. I turned to look back at them. She had reemerged into my life and had risen to become immaculate.

The overwhelming sense that my entire existence and purpose converged upon this very moment came over me. I wouldn't question it. I was simpatico with God and felt you must have made me for this.

This was real. I couldn't just let her go. I had to follow her. I brushed the snow off my pants and walked up the hill to the parking lot and sat inside my van, watching and waiting until the woman and her child appeared.

I followed them out of the parking lot as they drove off, feeling ashamed for being a stalker but I had no control.

"Man, it's not worth it. You've got to pull over and let them go," I said aloud. "Stop following them."

My heart was overpowering my intellect.

"Why am I doing this? What are you going to do, follow her home and knock on her door to introduce yourself?"

I hated this. This was not me. I'm not a stalker but I was like a fiend possessed. I wanted the angel to leave my body.

"Get out of me," I screamed.

"You were made to do this," a voice inside me said. "This is what you were born to do. You were born to connect with the Angel of Death and receive his consciousness."

I began to cry because I couldn't stop following them. I trailed them home and parked at a distance, watching them open their chain-link gate and go in. I would watch and wait.

It had been almost two hours of watching their house, sitting out in my van and crying, when I saw the side gate open and the little girl wander out into the street, kicking snow.

A man crossed her path. He wore a knit cap and an overcoat. He was holding a small cat. The little girl started to pet it and she went around the corner with him, leaving my sight. In my heart, I knew what was taking place. She was being abducted and you had placed me here to save her and to show her mother unconditional love by returning her safe. I was her destiny.

I sat there without urgency or emotion, waited for twenty seconds, started the van and drove slowly in the direction of where I believe them to have gone. I turned the corner as a grey Honda Civic pulled out with the little girl in the passenger seat. I slowed to let them gain some distance.

The sun was going down as the Civic headed out of town towards the river delta.

To avoid spooking the Civic's driver, I turned onto a side road, drove five blocks and then turned around, confident that I could pick up their trail in the fresh snow that covered the delta.

They were easy to find. I saw the Civic parked so I pulled up beside it and got out. I could see one set of tracks leading off into the wildlife reserve. The little girl was being carried off.

I went round to the back door of the van and grabbed the rope, t-ball bat and duct tape that I had bought five years ago. They were still there, the tools of destiny. Following the tracks in the snow, I didn't run or hurry but remained like you, calm and devoid of emotion.

Even though he'd taken a little girl, instead of a stripper, I knew I had found the Moth. We were in parallel.

I began to make an emotional estimation of his thoughts. He was impotent and trying something new in hopes of revitalizing himself.

"Still looking for your type?" I said. "Still can't get it up?"

After about a half mile, I spotted them on the river's edge. The Moth was so engrossed in his actions; he failed to notice me sneaking up from behind.

He was fondling the little girl with his right hand and restricting her movements with his left, doing things that I best not describe. The child was limp with fear.

I stood over them, studying the situation as the heat of the moment veiled me from their attention. I wondered if this was what it was like for my sister? Possibly, but unlike Amanda, the Moth intended this little girl to rest on the river's floor.

At ease, I slowly lifted the bat and brought it down, cracking the fiend's skull. He lay limp in the snow. The little girl stayed on her back, looking up at me, trembling. I pulled her out from under him.

"Do you know who this is?" I pointed with the bat to the bleeding pervert.

The little girl just stared at me, trying not to cry.

"He's the Moth. He kills people. Do you have a name?"

She wouldn't answer. The chill from the river cut through me so I knew she must be cold.

"I've saved your life," I said, sternly, pointing the bloody bat at her face. "Do you understand?"

She nodded.

"If you are thankful, then you won't tell anyone about me or what I look like. Though I've helped you, I'm a very bad man. Do you promise?"

She nodded and began to cry. "Now run for your life. Go to the road."

The little girl ran away from me.

I looked down at the Moth, his blood staining the snow like cherry red. I kicked him over with my boot.

It was Steve Jahl.

CHAPTER 36

I DIDN'T EXPECT Steve to be the Moth but I wasn't necessarily surprised. It couldn't have been coincidence. Our lives ran in tandem. Right here, right now, we were each other's destiny and he was proof that I was not crazy.

Looking down at his limp body, hearing the little Jehovah Witness girl's boots crushing the snow as she ran, I knew that my past disdain for God was not disbelief but denial that kept me from achieving my two foremost desires, marrying Lily and killing her brother. But here I was, with Steve at my mercy and I had found a love far better than that of his sister. If you can submit to the divine, life is perfect.

I looked down at Steve and knew that he was still among the living. I took the duct tape and bound his arms and legs, covering his mouth; fastened the rope to his feet and drug him through the snow.

Within five minutes I came across the little girl crying. She was apparently lost.

"Please mister, help me."

"Come on," I said, dragging Steve along behind, the

rope that bound his feet slung over my shoulder. "Follow me."

"Are you going to kill him, mister?"

I stopped and turned to her.

"It's our destiny, all three of us. He and I must die so you can live. It was ordained along time ago. I don't know who you are but you must be one special little girl. God loves you and has sent me to protect you. This I know."

I put Steve into the back of the van and drove to the edge of the little girl's neighborhood.

"Go home," I said. "Don't tell anyone about me until Christmas morning, then you can tell your mom what you've seen. Tell her that in an ideal world, I could have loved her, maybe even been your daddy. Tell her that your safe return is my gift to her. Tell her that I'm the angel Samael."

I watched her run down the street into her house. It was getting late and I'm sure she'd been missed. I engaged drive and headed to the mountain.

The last time I'd been up to the mountain was that day I dug Steve's grave and got pneumonia. The sun had now set, giving me the privacy I needed.

I opened the back door, looking at Steve, knowing that my dreams of youth, to rise above adversity, to fall in love and marry a thick-legged girl and have a kid or just to be wealthy, healthy and defy old age, were all gone. Did they mean anything, anyway?

With a pull, Steve's body fell on the snow covered asphalt. I looked around at the darkened houses. Everyone was inside, keeping warm. Only you knew of my intentions.

Would Steve's grave still be there? It didn't matter. I took a deep breath and with Steve in tow, began to climb. When I had climbed for about thirty yards, I looked to my left and noticed the Mormon Temple down below in the town.

Perched on its turret was a statue of the angel Moroni, watching me from the distance, his golden stare, devoid of judgment or emotion.

I thought of the kid that gave me the Book of Mormon.

"Holiness to the Lord, the house of the Lord," I said.

I began to sweat profusely, pulling Steve up the steep grade. Though the snow made it easier for me to slide him, the exertion was becoming too much for me. I could feel my muscles ripping as I forced myself to continue, pushing all doubts about my course of action out of my mind. My only thoughts were about making that ledge, where I had dug that grave so many years before.

My clothes were damp with sweat and my chest heaving so I stopped to rest. Resuming my climb, I couldn't fathom how I had gotten as far as I had come. Soon adrenaline filled my ripped core and I was able to progress in my ascent.

"Why?" I screamed to you and the heavens. "God, why me? Go fuck yourself, you bitch."

When I finally reached the plateau, I collapsed next to Steve and put my hand on my chest to try and calm my breathing. Looking around, I saw everything was just as I had left it over five years ago: the rock, the hole- even my shovel, all rusted, was still resting against the edge of the pit.

I propped Steve up in the hole and began to fill the pit with dirt. As the first shovel full of dirt hit Steve's face, I could hear thunder in the distance. Its bass frequencies were of such power that I could almost feel it. Beads of sweat began to pour down my face as I shoveled with all my might.

Within twenty minutes I was able to exert enough energy to bury Steve alive from the neck down. His unconscious appearance was horrible. I had loved this man's sister so I fell to my knees and began to weep.

"God, what can I do? Who can help me?"

All I could think of was you.

"Forgive me for everything I have done. What's

become of my life?" I sobbed in hysterics for some time.

"I need help," I said, snot and tears dripping down my chin.

But whom can anyone turn to in such times?

"Oh God," I said to the sky. "I love you and believe in you and I'm sorry. I accept my fate. I am one of your eagles, paying homage to you as I fly into the sun. And only you can set me upon a path that will enable me to realize my full potential.

"This is what you have done for me all along and I was ungrateful. But it hasn't been easy. If you could just ease the burden a little, I would forever love you and be in your debt. I shall love you long after the world's beauty has faded, for you are beyond imperfection. It's made it so I can die happy, knowing that for the past five years, I have dedicated my life to you."

I lay my back against the rock that would serve as Steve's headstone and napped until the twilight roused me. I stood and put my boot down next to Steve's head, looking up into the sun as it rose, forcing myself to stare and not squint. I stayed true, looking into the burning glare.

"I believe," I shouted and I did.

You do exist and within the blinding fury, I could see your face, it was what I saw when I looked into the aura and inner soul of the stripper girl. I could see God.

I knelt down and pulled the duct tape from Steve's mouth, causing him to moan. I became distracted by the sounds of his coming to.

"What's going on? Where am I?"

"Shut up," I snarled.

"Who are you?"

He didn't recognize me. I stood up and kicked his head with all my might.

"Why have you brought me here?" He was deathly afraid.

"To watch you die."

He began to sob. "I still don't know who you are."

"You raped my sister." I had my back to him,

watching the rising sun.

"Good God, you're Samael Giltine. Look Sam, I'm sorry. I need help."

"No, you need to die," I said, turning back to glare at him.

"It's not my fault. I can't help it, I'm the victim."

"Fuck you." I stood up and walked up to him, grabbing his hair to tilt his stare into mine.

"Look Samael, you had the hots for Lily. I could hook you up."

"I can no longer express mortal love. I'm a servant of God." I spit on his face.

"It's not my fault Sam. If you believe in God, at least listen to me."

"Ok," I said. "Let's hear it. Why should I let you live?"

He took some time to orient his defense. "I'm a victim. When I was a kid, I was molested."

"By your father?"

"No, by my mother."

"Emily? Doesn't surprise me. I always knew it. Most folks thought it was Dan."

"He was mean and would hit me but he doesn't know about me. He still thinks I'm not guilty of everything I've done."

"That's because he's fucking stupid. You are guilty. If I hadn't been there, that little girl would be dead and buried in the mire by now."

Steve began crying out for his momma.

"You piece of shit," I yelled, punting him on the side of his head with the steel toe of my boot.

"Please don't kill me. Just turn me in to the police. They'll send me to prison."

"What, so you can get sodomized and become someone's bitch, get room and board, medical provided free? I don't think so. That'd be a paradise for a pervert like you."

"I promise to reform. I'll never do it again."

"You've got the taste. Once you've had it on your lips, there's no turning back. Believe me, I know."

"That's not true. It's always better as fantasy," he said.

I looked at him in horror. "What are you talking about?"

"You can check out porn on video and its always better," he said, just a head sticking above the soil. "Porn loses something when you take it to the level of reality."

At this point, I wanted to hear what he had to say. "What do you mean?" I asked.

"When I killed those women, it wasn't what I thought it would be."

"What you mean, is that you couldn't get a hard on after you'd slit their throats?"

He looked away in shame. "Yes."

"So you switch to little girls so maybe you'll be able to get off? You sick fuck. You had no problem cumming in my sister."

I kicked him in the head again. He must have feared the reprimand of my boot and went silent. For three hours I sat staring at him, watching him suffer.

"Any last words?"

"I don't want to die." His cheeks were turning bluish-purple from the cold. "I don't want to be like me. I try to stop. Sometimes I go for a long time, controlling it but sometimes I can't help myself. It's like I'm being pulled. It's as if someone or something is controlling me. I just can't stop."

I looked to the ground in a haze, wondering about my own life, about how other men were daily striving to shed their animal instincts and become more civilized. Steve and I had failed in this quest.

We're animals, but animals loved by God. I am an eagle and he is the moth. But I am determined to end in grace. My life is such a disaster; a black cloud follows me. By starting to hunt this predator, all those years ago, I have assumed his form.

"Are we not men?" I stared at my hands. "Are we not men?"

I heard sirens off in the town and stepped up onto the ridge of the basin to look down to the houses below. I could see my mom's house in the distance; a long stream of police cars was converging on it from all directions.

"What is it?" asked Steve.

"They've come for me but I'm not there."

"Come for you?" he said, confused.

"Yes, for me."

"Why would they come for you?"

"Because, they call me the Back Alley Killer. I have killed eight people and you are about to be my ninth victim."

I stepped back into the basin, away from view, walking over to Steve. He grew silent, looking back at me.

"You know," I said, standing above his head, poking out of the ground, "I don't fully understand yet but I am beginning to see that evil is a necessary function of the universe. Without it, there can be no good. I am part of this function."

I knelt down to be close to Steve's face. "Unfortunately this leads me to this question: should I kill you or set you free?"

He swallowed. "What's your answer?"

"I have to ask God, for unlike you, I was never given free will."

CHAPTER 37

STANDING ON THE tip of the basin, I watched the police cars race their way towards the mountain. Only some of the cars had converged on my mother's, the rest were making their way up to me. I wondered how they knew where to go. Who knows? It didn't matter.

The police cars had a certain beauty, inching smoothly towards me, equidistant apart, lights shimmering like spinning wheels on the tree of life.

I suppose the sounds would have bothered me but I could no longer hear the cacophony of this world, only the silence of my mind. I looked back to Steve. He was shouting at me but I could not hear his pleas.

It was time. I reached into my pocket and realized I had dropped my grandfather's knife on the shores of the Spokane River Delta. I would have to use the rusted shovel. I stepped into the basin and slowly picked it up, inspecting it, as if it knew the answer.

"Am I Samael Giltine or the Angel of Death?"

"You're Samael," said Steve.

I could read his thoughts, his lips.

"I am Samael. But there is a part of me, deep within,

that is the angel. I am both good and evil. Some angels live in the wind. Wind can destroy. Some reside in water. They can quench your thirst or drown your children. Despite our various functions, we angels are all guardians, perched on our watchtowers with cherubic wings to soar on high."

"Angels don't kill people, Samael."

"You're wrong about that. I should be chopping your head with a flaming sword, not a rusted shovel."

I looked him in the eye and rammed the shovel, just under his chin, with all my might.

I always thought I'd murder Steve slow, nothing crude or hasty. But it ended up being quite vulgar in the end, lacking any semblance of the beauty that embodied my earlier art. By the time the shovel had pierced his skin the angel had left me and I was once again just plain old Sam.

It took a little time to hack off his head. It eventually came off and I knelt down to pick it up from the puddle of bloody mud to hold it above me.

I looked back into the sun. Again, you were there.

"Sam," you said, "it's time to come home."

"I'll be there soon."

I looked down the mountainside. Cops and dogs were making their way up the hill through the snow. Special Agent Broderick was in the lead, desperate to secure the prey that had been slipping through his fingers. He could catch me but his game would not be won.

I was at peace. My life's purpose had been fulfilled and I was ready to go home.

Broderick slowed to a walk as he neared me. His gun remained holstered. He instinctively knew he would not need it. We stood looking at each other, surrounded by law enforcement officers pointing their guns.

"Hello Sam," he said.

I'll never forget the sound of his voice or the look on his face as he pointed to the head that I held in my hands. "Is that the Moth?"

I nodded.

My attorney used schizophrenia as defense to avoid the death penalty. But when I was examined by the state, they found no trace of any sort of mania. I was found completely sane. The angel was gone and so was the voice of God.

Last night was nice. It was the night before my execution and my last hours on earth. Your spirit held me in your arms as we lay on the cot in my jail cell, knowing that whatever I have done, you would still love me. You kissed my cheek; gently stroking my hair, telling me you'd meet me on the other side.

"I'll be wearing the same red tank top and black skirt I wore when you first saw me."

"Will you wear your rollerblades?"

"If you'd like."

"I'd like that, thank you."

You held my face with both of your hands and kissed my lips.

"I have to go now. They're coming for you. Always remember, I love you."

You disappeared into the ethereal night. A buzzer sounded, followed by the mechanics of my prison latch. In came Special Agent Broderick, holding a folder, followed by a priest.

"Sam," he said. "I wanted to personally say goodbye to you. A priest is here if you want to offer confession."

I smiled and shook my head. "It won't be necessary. I've made my peace."

"Are you refusing confession?" said the priest.

"Yes. But thank you anyway."

He left. Broderick opened his folder.

"That night at Fort Spokane, when the Moth struck upriver in Hunters, I thought you might want to know who his last victim was."

He handed me an 8x10 photo. It was you, my stripper Avatar of God.

I held it, looking into your eyes. There was no divine light coming from the photo, nothing special, just a girl who had been killed. You and I were two ethereal beings, trapped in our bodies, not sure how to maneuver through this life.

God had departed the body, leaving the rotten core, an empty shell of a drug addicted stripper.

It had to be you. It could be no other.

"She lived in LA at the time you committed your killings. She moved to Seattle about the same time you returned to Fairdemidland. She had gone back to visit her family. We found your DNA on her. You knew her, didn't you?"

Broderick was looking at me with pathos. I nodded, handing him back his photo. "I'm about to join her."

ABOUT THE AUTHOR

Prolific author, lyricist and poet, Brandon Pitts infuses his creations with the experience of a life lived on the edge. From the jungles of Cambodia to the back alleys of Los Angeles, his work penetrates the darker side of spirituality, balancing the sublime with the grotesque. In 2011, he was selected for inclusion in the prestigious Diaspora Dialogues as an Emerging Voice and is the author of the poetry collection *Pressure to Sing*. Brandon lives in Toronto, Ontario. *Puzzle of Murders* is his first novel. For additional information about Brandon Pitts please visit his website www.brandonpitts.com.

ACKNOWLEDGEMENTS

I would like to thank the following people who helped with the creation of this book. My mother, for believing in me so much that she offered to support me during a writing sabbatical in which this novel was written. My father and his lovely wife CJ, for their endless support and belief in what I do. Brian Henry, for his invaluable critique of the manuscript. My good friends Shawna Andrews and Robin Keifer-Mclaren, who test read a very rough first draft. Cal, who also test read the manuscript. My lovely partner, Iddie Fourka aka Tallulah Doll, who test read the edited draft. Greg Lawson, for coming out of retirement to shoot my picture for the book. Jasmine D'Costa, for being the best mentor a writer could have. Nik Beat and Norman Cristofoli, for promoting me as a writer and poet. Those who published me when no one else would: *Labour of Love, Conceit Magazine, BookLand Press, Trade Architects* and *Quick Brown Fox*. Sherry Isaac, for teaching me how to do what needs be done. Saskia van Tetering, for invaluable friendship as a fellow writer. Mary-Ellen Koroscil, whose encouragement gave me confidence to step up. And last but not least, editorial staff of BookLand Press, for believing in me and taking the time to answer all my questions.